THE HUSSY AND THE HARDCASE

The Hardcase Vol. 1

JACK R. STANLEY

Wrightbridge Press

The Hussy and the Hardcase
Copyright © 2020 by Jack R. Stanley.
All rights reserved.
ISBN: 978-1-947726-92-5

This book may not be copied or reproduced, in whole or in part, by any means, electronic, mechanical or otherwise, without written permission from the publisher except by a reviewer who may quote brief passages in his/her review.
This is a work of fiction. Any resemblance to any persons, events or localities is purely coincidental and beyond the intent of the author and publisher.

Credits:

Cover by
Kevin Diamond

Edited by
Mary Lee Stanley
and
Rose Marie Reed

Wrightbridge Press
jacks@wrightbridgepress.com
www.thefictionwritersnotebook.com
www.jackrstanley.com

To the love of my life
Mary Lee
who makes all things possible.

And to
Mitchel Whitington
Travel writer, historian, and friend.

TWO FREE E-BOOKS

[Murder in Muleshoe]
If you were murdered would they try to find the killer or plan him a parade?

[Guns Along The Rio]
In 1858, two fresh-off-the-ranch 17-year-olds join the Texas Rangers. What could possibly go wrong?

GO TO: http://eepurl.com/dKEi_Y

CHAPTER 1

Boyd Spanner connected with a left cross to the side of Thrope Gains's massive block of a head. It was like punching a block of granite. The blow staggered the bigger man, but it also sent shock waves up Boyd's arm. He could have followed with a right to Thrope's face and most likely drawn blood, but that wasn't the point of this exercise. And he wasn't worried about scrambling the killer and stage robber's brains. That omelet had been baked in by the Texas sun years before.

Boyd let Thorpe rock back, regain his balance, and shook off the impact of the punch. When he was ready, Thorpe would come for Boyd. He'd be madder than a wounded bear and have everything he had behind each swing of his monolithic arms.

The man was 6 foot 6, and all 280 pounds of it were muscle. Boyd's first day in prison, he knew he'd eventually have to slug it out with this monster. Thorpe was ignorant and a bully. Boyd stayed away from him and out of the ogre's way.

This was Boyd's last day in lockup, and he knew Thorpe would be coming for him. Thorpe had 2 inches and about 30 pounds on Boyd — maybe more. Prison took a toll on every man — Boyd figured he'd dropped at least 20 pounds. Cutting Texas sugarcane on a chain gang along the Brazos kept a man's muscles in shape, but the prison food was never enough.

The guards stood back behind the circle of convicts allowing the fight to happen. Even those with shotguns high on the walls and in the towers were watching with interest. No one was going to interrupt this contest.

Boyd had never been any problem to the guards. But he didn't make friends with them either. The man understood from the first day that prison was an us vs. them-world, and the guards were "them."

From the bulls' point-of-view, either Thorpe might just get what had been coming to him for years, or they'd pitch Boyd out the front door tomorrow battered, bruised if he was still alive. Either way, the guards felt they were winners.

For Boyd Spanner, prison was a setback. After the war, which he entered when he was 16, he had come West hoping to make something of his life — to somehow make up for the killer he felt he had become in the Army.

Boyd's father was killed in the first year of the war at the Battle of Big Bethel. It took place on the Virginia Peninsula, near Newport News. Union soldiers attacked a Confederate position near a church. The Union forces were repelled. Because of how his father was killed, defending a church, Boyd always thought of the war as The War Of Northern Aggression.

Boyd lied about his age and joined the army. He was a natural shot and became a sniper. He didn't returned to his Georgia home until after Appomattox. He discovered his mother was dead and the home place had been burned to the ground. He headed West.

Boyd side stepped Thorpe's bull rush and clipped the big man's boots, causing him to stumble into the dirt. Thorpe regained his feet and came at Boyd in a blind rage, throwing wild almost roundhouse blows, which Boyd avoided leaving only damaged air in the wake of each angry swing.

Ducking under one of them, Boyd stepped behind Thorpe and used both arms to jam an elbow into one of Thorpe's kidneys. This brought a scream of pain from Thorpe.

Thorpe's hands were like bricks, and Boyd knew better than to be where they landed. When the anger-driven man had tried his bull rush a second time, Boyd didn't move until the very last second when he grabbed Thorpe's ragged shirt and dropped to his back and planting both feet into the bully's gut. As Boyd rocked back, he clutched the stage hold-up killer's tattered shirt and pushed with all the strength in his legs. The result was that Thorpe was vertical like an upright poll before Boyd released his hold and allowed gravity and the colossal goon's weight to slam the giant headfirst into the ground. There was a cracking sound as all of Thorpe's heft accumulated on his skull.

Boyd got to his feet and waited as Thorpe struggled to roll over and stand again on wobbly columns of leg muscles. Blood streamed down Thorpe's face and into his eyes. He wiped dirt into his eyes, trying to clear away the blood.

The smaller man flipped over on his hands, and again, using both legs, mule kicked Thorpe in the chest. Once more, the goon staggered, but he didn't fall. Boyd circled the hulk to avoid the now awkward blows Thorpe threw. Thorpe howled and thrashed at each elbow Boyd drove into the staggering beast. Boyd kept out of reach and delivered jabs to the big man's face breaking his nose.

But in a surprising move, Thorpe was able to grab Boyd and lift him off the ground in a bear hug. Thorpe wanted to use his strength to break Boyd's ribs, if not his back. Boyd slapped both of Thorpe's ears with every ounce of the power he had. Thorpe was quickly turning the hug into a body vice grip.

Thorpe dropped Boyd and stepped back, cupping his bleeding ears and bending forward. Boyd used the opening to crash his right knee into Thorpe's head, using his hands to hold the man's skull for the full impact.

Thorpe dropped like a wet bag of red mud and only moved to draw his breath in gasps.

One of the guards, a towering black man with a truncheon in his hand, stepped through the gathered convicts and clubbed Boyd from behind. Another guard rushed forward, and together they pulled the winner away. They assigned four prisoners to lug Boyd to the infirmary.

Money changed hands between most of the guards as Boyd was carried away. A group of Thorpe's minions tried to help their leader.

* * *

Two guards escorted Boyd from the infirmary to the out-processing station. He massaged the bruise on his neck, where it met his shoulder. One of the guards laughed.

"That may hurt for a day or two, but believe me, Shadow saved your life, hardcase. Those other yard birds would have killed you for what you did to Thorpe. He's the king of the yard — and you put him down like a poleaxed ox."

"Thank Mr. Shadow for me," Boyd said, trying to roll his injured shoulder and winced as he did. "He does good work."

The guards laughed.

Boyd took a box from another guard through a window ledge in a cage. It contained the boots and clothes he wore the day he entered prison. He sat on a bench and changed his clothes from his prison rags to a black suit, vest, white shirt, and decent boots he only vaguely remembered. Nothing fit him right. He had lost too much weight. But he dressed anyway.

"There's somebody waiting for you," the other guard told Boyd when he finally stood in his civilian clothes. "You expecting someone?"

"Lady Justice on a big white horse," Boyd said. "Maybe Lady Godiva."

"Then you're going to be disappointed," the other guard said.

The guards ushered Boyd to the tall wooden door. Using a key, the first guard unlocked a smaller door and swung it outward.

"Try not to come back," the second guard said as Boyd stepped into the sunshine and put on his hat. "Feel free to rent out my cell," he said.

The door slammed closed, and the lock clicked.

Boyd recognized the man mounted on the bay. It was his business partner, Layman Haverstick. Together they owned The Bale of Cotton saloon up in Jefferson.

"You didn't expect to see me," Layman said.

"I didn't expect to see anyone."

Boyd couldn't see Layman's bald head since the man wore a flat-brimmed hat. He was clean-shaven, one golden tooth at the top center of his jaw. He wore a suit and an old but serviceable gunbelt. Layman offered the bridal to the swayback, saddled dun to the newly released man. "Welcome back to life," Layman said sincerely.

"Where's my horse?" Boyd asked.

"She's well taken care of. We just wanted to ensure you come back for her. If I'd of brought her, you might mount up and simply ride away."

"You take the nag," Boyd said, refusing the offered reins. "I'll ride the bay."

"Don't be like that."

"Get down," Boyd ordered, taking hold of the bay's reins.

Layman Haverstick dismounted. "I was afraid you'd do something like this."

CHAPTER 2

"Was that nag a prize for last place in something?" Boyd asked Layman Haverstick.

"He could be yours if you want. Same thing with the saddle and all the tack. Take it all and ride away if you like?"

"Where's my appaloosa?"

"Arch Lamp's got her at his livery. He's got your tack, too. Been takin' good care of it all."

"Why?" Boyd said, mounting the bay.

"We all know you got a raw deal, Boyd. Godfrey Mull needed killin' for a long time. Nobody else had the nerve t' do it. Then you did."

"And it cost me 3 years cutting cane."

"That was Judge Tewilliker. We all testified on your side. You remember that, don't you? And the jury found you innocent. Tewilliker overruled everybody. He said even a pimp's life is worth something. It was Tewilliker that sent you to prison. He's been in hell for most of the time you've been locked up. Kicked the bucket a month or two after he sent you down."

"What is it you're expecting of me?" Boyd asked.

"Not a thing. You don't owe me or Jefferson a thing. Fact is, I owe you — your half of the profits while you've been locked up."

"I didn't expect ever to see any of that." Boyd kicked the bay lightly and headed North.

"Where are you goin'," Layman asked.

"Where do you think — partner?"

"It's almost a 3-day ride."

"Then let's get on with it."

"I ain't sleeping on the ground. I'm too old and too fat." Layman had enough of a paunch to keep him from seeing his feet when he was standing up. He urged his nag on South. "You comin'?"

Boyd stopped and looked over his shoulder. "What do you suggest?"

"Port Arthur first. Sheriff Danforth's waiting for us. He's got your guns and some of your money. He's also got us tickets on a boat to New Orleans."

"New Orleans?"

"We'll take a freighter to there. Then we'll pick up a riverboat there and go home by the river."

"That's going to take two — could be three weeks?"

"It also means beds, restaurants. You in a hurry, Boyd?"

Boyd considered the options and decided the idea of going by boat wasn't a bad idea at all.

The barkeep started out alone. But Boyd eased around and was soon beside Layman headed for Port Arthur.

* * *

At Port Arthur, Boyd and Layman Haverstick met Sheriff Corwin Danforth. The 60-year-old lawman was freckled with thinning blonde hair that curled over his ears. He wore a brown leather vest with his star pinned on it. A pocket watch was in his right vest pocket, and a gold chain hung across his slightly bludging mid-drift to a pocket knife in his other pocket. He was what folks called "big-boned," meaning he was hefty but not fat.

"Layman," the Sheriff greeted Haverstick as the saloon owner led his swayback nag aboard a rusty freighter named The Hamlet. "See he swapped horses with you," Corwin laughed. "At least you were able to convince him to come with you?"

"A hell of a choice," Boyd said, following with the bay in tow.

"We wanted you to come back," the Sheriff said to Boyd, "and I wasn't sure you ever wanted to see Jefferson again."

"I'm still half owner of The Bale of Cotton — and a few other businesses. Not all my memories are fond."

"Oh, I get it," Sheriff Danforth said, walking with the pair down the ramp. "But that also means you have investments in the town. What happens to it should concern you."

"You've got some money for me?" Boyd asked.

"Some," the Sheriff pulled a pouch out of the inside pocket of his vest. He handed it to Boyd. The contents jingled as Boyd hefted it.

"There's also some foldin' money in there, too. The rest is in Asberry Kropp's bank. I do have your pistol and your Winchester, but in my room onboard. Both are clean and in good condition. I've been using saddle soap on your leather and keeping your hardware oiled up. And here are your tickets to New Orleans. Your room number is on them."

A few minutes later, up in Sheriff Danforth's room, the lawman handed Boyd back his holster, his converted Remington '61 Army, and his Winchester rifle. Boyd liked the revolver because he had it reworked by a gunsmith despite it being manufactured as a cap and ball style weapon. Now it accepted metal cartridges. It also used the same caliber ammunition as his rifle.

The three of them ate supper in the ship's mess after they had cast off. The meal was beef stew, and Boyd had two helpings. He surprised the cook by telling the oriental man that his chow was good. The best, he said, he'd had in three years. Few crewmen or passengers even spoke to the cook, much less praised his efforts.

The seas were calm, and Boyd, Layman, and Sheriff Corwin Danforth had an after dinner smoke up on deck.

"Okay," Boyd said after a few moments, "what's this all about? Drop the other boot."

"What do you mean?" Danforth asked as innocently as he could manage.

"You're not in the habit of meeting ex-cons and escorting them back to town, Corwin. So what is really going on here?"

"Right to the point, aren't you, Boyd?" the Sheriff asked. "You ever take the easy way — around about — ease into things?"

"Not my way. Now, what is it you've not been telling me?"

The Sheriff and Layman Haverstick exchanged looks, and the lawman sighed before he began.

"We want you to run for sheriff of Marion County."

Boyd laughed out loud — paused — looked at both his business partner and the Sheriff and roared again.

"When in hell am I anybody's best friend in town? Who even talks to me who doesn't have to?"

"You remember Vander Osby?" Layman asked.

"The carpetbagger? Loudmouth, egg suckin' scalawag?"

"That's him."

"I thought he'd be gone with the rest of the reconstructionist trash by now?"

"Not Vander. He's decided he likes our town. Made himself a fixture of sorts. And reconstruction isn't over. It's eased — but it's not over."

"So?"

"We hear he's decided to run for Sheriff next election?" Danforth said.

"You're the Sheriff, Corwin. You ready to retire or something?"

"I ain't' gettin' any younger."

"Who is? Try spending three years cutting cane on a chain gang."

"Don't be such a hard ass, Boyd."

"I think I've paid my dues to society. I don't owe Jefferson a damn thing!"

"No, you don't, and nobody's sayin' you do."

"Then don't be askin' me stupid questions. I have no love for the law — and I'm not that pleased with Jefferson."

"You got another job offer?"

"I don't need one. I own half of The Bale, and I'm a gambler. I'll get along."

"Maybe you will — but — damn it, Boyd, this is somethin' you can do. Somethin' you ought to do."

"Why in the hell should I?"

"I have faith in you, Boyd. Although right this minute, I'm not really thrilled about feelin' that way. You showed yourself to be — first of all, a hardcase — a pain in the ass — and at times, you make me so mad I wouldn't piss on you if you caught fire." The Sheriff took a breath before he continued, "But damn you, Boyd, you're fair and honest. I've seen you lose your shirt and get up and walk away from the table without a complaint. And for all your faults — and I think you've got more than most — you have what it takes to be a good lawman."

"I just got out of prison today. How can you say that?"

"See," the saloon co-owner said to Corwin, "I told you so."

"Nobody like t' hear that, Layman. And it's not helpin'." The Sheriff shook his head at Layman before turning back to Boyd. "Here's the deal. I'm gettin' long in the tooth — and I need t' retire. If Vander Osby runs, nobody will run against him. We all know what that would mean to Jefferson and the whole county."

Boyd stared at Corwin.

"Okay, you're getting old. Happens to us all. I'm about a decade older than I was when you arrested me — at least I feel that way. But me — a convict as a sheriff?"

"That would not normally be the case, but — you didn't murder Godfrey Mull. Yes, you shot the som'bitch and killed him, but that was like puttin' down a rabid dog. Needed t' be done. Everybody around town knows it."

"I reminded him about the jury all bein' on his side," Layman said.

"Anything else?" Boyd asked almost with a laugh.

CHAPTER 3

Boyd Spanner, Sheriff Corwin Danforth, and Boyd's co-owner of The Bale of Cotton saloon, Layman Haverstick, talked on the deck of The Hamlet, a freight steamer out of Port Arthur headed for New Orleans.

Sheriff Danforth took a deep breath before continuing his argument that Boyd should be Marian County's next sheriff. "Yes, there is something else. You're not a hothead — and you've got what it takes t' do what needs doin'."

Boyd was shaking his head, but no words were coming out of his mouth.

"Look, here," Sheriff Danforth said, "don't say 'No' right now. This is somethin' you never expected. I get that. But give it a week or two. It's kind of a slow trip up the river t' home. Think about it. Maybe you don't need a job, but folks in Jefferson and the whole county need you. You don't have a job and, okay, you don't need one. All right, I understand. But this could be a good deal for you. You'd get $300 a month plus fines and rewards — that could come in handy if you have a terrible run of luck at the table. You could get yourself a deputy and wouldn't have to do that much work. With your name behind the badge, Boyd, it would keep the likes of Vander Osby and his kind in line.

"And one more thing. The Excelsior House — still the best hotel in town is willing to provide you with a room as part of the job."

When Boyd didn't say no, it was quiet on the deck.

"Just think about it. Get you some new clothes in New Orleans and enjoy the ride back home. The election isn't for two months."

That was the end of the conversation, and both Sheriff Danforth and Layman Haverstick took that as a good sign.

* * *

In New Orleans, Boyd did get himself two new suits, shirts, and underwear. He also got him a new Stetson. He decided he didn't need boots but had the ones he wore shined almost until they sparkled.

Sheriff Danforth had gotten the three men rooms for the night. Boyd buoyed by Bourbon Street's nightlife. He got in a poker game, but he walked away about even with what he had when he sat down after a couple of hours. He could still read men, but his big, calloused hands weren't as adept with cards as they had been.

He didn't see either the Sheriff or Layman that day. That night, however, when he checked into the hotel room, the clerk handed him a ticket for The Chapel Hill pushing off the next morning at 8 o'clock.

He slept better in the hotel than he had on The Hamlet. Boyd wasn't sure if it was because of the better bed in the hotel or his getting used to not sleeping on a straw pad over rigid boards he'd gotten used to.

At the front desk, Boyd checked out but took his new grip with the new clothes he wasn't wearing to the dining room. After a moment's thought, he spotted his traveling companions and decided to join them for breakfast.

When they were finished, Layman said, "You keep eatin' like that an' you'll end up fat like me."

"Not likely," Boyd said without a smile.

As he laid the price of his meal and a generous tip for the pretty Irish waitress, he said to Danforth, "I only left $200 on the table back in Jefferson," Boyd said. "Where'd all this that money you gave me come from? It isn't mine."

"See there? You are an honest man," the lawman grinned.

"One of my many faults."

"No, it's all yours."

"Some of it is your share of The Bale since you've been gone," Layman said, wiping his chin and paying his own share of the bill.

"It's at least what you would have made of it if it hadn't been for the shooting. 'Compound interest,' Asberry Kropp calls it. And don't ask who contributed to it 'cause I ain't sayin'."

Boyd tightened his jaw, sighed, and pocketed the coins in his hand.

* * *

They boarded The Chapel Hill, an impressive paddle wheeler, at the dock, and each man had a stateroom. For two days, they worked their way up the Mississippi, stopping to take on or let off passengers and freight. Folks on the riverbank would flag them down at a landing stop, or the Captain knew where to stop for those leaving the boat.

At Shreveport, located near Lousiana's top left-hand corner, where the Red River joins the Mississippi, the trio got off The Chapel Hill. It was headed on up to St. Louis, but they were going up the Cypress River. The trio, their horses, and bags were transferred to a smaller boat, The Quintana II. They followed the twisting Cypress River Northwest through the bayous and swamps. They passed through Caddo Lake by holding to the center channel. The lake was filled with underwater logs and snags that would sink a shallow draft paddle-wheeler. Caddo Indians and the hearty Texans who lived around the swamps and bayous commonly caught gars as long as an arm. And there were tales of Big Bill, a huge and ancient alligator. Tales of Big Bill were told to naughty children to frighten them into better behavior.

Sheriff Danforth and Layman Haverstick kept to themselves and out of Boyd's way. He became a regular in the salons and gambling table. Little by little, his old skills with cards returned. By the time the boat docked, he had added $400 to his purse.

* * *

It was coming on to dusk when they arrived at Jefferson "Riverport to the Southwest." Most say the city of Jefferson was named after the third U.S. President. But arguments could begin by saying that. It was nearly 170 miles east of Dallas.

The town was founded around 1841 on land ceded from the Caddo Indians. It was a major cotton and armaments shipping point during the War of Nothern Aggression. It was a thriving port with about 20,000 residents the summer evening Boyd Spanner and Layman Haverstick and Sheriff Corwin Danforth arrived.

Two other steamers were tied up to the wharf when The Quintana II pulled in. Laborers were already tossing bundles from the ship to waiting hands on the doc.

"Why are they wasting decks of cards on the cargo?" Boyd askes as the boat was being secured. A single card was attached to each parcel and load. Boyd had noticed it days before and had been wondering.

"Most of these rousteabouts can't read," Danforth said, "but they can play cards. Jefferson is the King of Spades."

CHAPTER 4

Up Polk Street, a couple of blocks from the dock was Arch Lamp's livery. Boyd and Haverstick turned in their rented horses, too. As Boyd handed over the reins to the bay he'd taken from his business partner, Layman, the liveryman, said, "Welcome home, Boyd. It's good t' see ya'."

"Yeah," said Boyd, with no enthusiasm.

Arch Lamp wore bib overalls and was a string bean of a man. When Layman handed over the reins to the swayback, Boyd's partner said, "This one is ready for the glue factory."

"He got you where you were goin', didn't he?"

"Barely. I expected him to drop dead with each step he took."

"Ol' Stonewall still got lots of miles in him," Arch said, patting the animal on the neck and scratched his own two-week growth of brown and grey beard. "Jest 'cause somebody's old don't mean they're worn out."

Boyd found his appaloosa in excellent health. The animal recognized Boyd and responded to her owner.

"How much do I owe you, Arch?" Boyd asked.

"Not a thing."

"You workin' for free these days?"

"Have you ever known me to do that?" the livery owner said, turning both rented horses into his corral.

"As I remember you, Arch," Boyd said, "you could squeeze silver out of a wooden nickel."

"A man's got t' make a livin'."

"So how come I don't owe you anything for taking care of my horse for 3 years?"

"Anonymous citizens from Jefferson," Sheriff Danforth said.

"Anonymous?" Boyd asked.

"Remember the Sheriff told you not to ask," Haverstick answered.

Boyd took Arch Lamp's hand and shook it. "Well, at least I can say, thank you, Arch."

"Paid in full," the scrawny man grinned. "But now that you're back, standard rates apply."

* * *

The Excelsior House Hotel was on Austin street, near the docks. By far, it was one of the best in town. The Kahn right up the street, had a good reputation, too, but it was known to be the hang out for those in the Klan. The rooms in The Excelsior were spacious, comfortable, and clean. Sheets were changed twice a week, and the hotel's dining room was first class.

After enjoying a bath of his life, Boyd slept in a bed, although with trouble. Even the weeks on the riverboat didn't prepare him for the scrubbed and aroma night air of the Texas piney woods. He did feel like he was home.

* * *

The next morning Boyd's first stop was Kropp Bank. The 40-some-odd-year-old red-haired banker always dressed in a suit. Boyd had often thought the man looked more like an undertaker than a banker. Asberry Kropp welcomed Boyd into his wood-paneled office and offered him a comfortable chair.

Kropp pulled a 5-inch square notebook with a leather cover and the

Kropp Bank stamp branded on the surface from his desk. The banker sat back and cleaned his spectacles with a white handkerchief. Boyd found his name inside the little books. It listed a series of deposits beginning about the time he was hauled off to prison. There were regular deposits and some interest additions. The amount at the end astonished Boyd, who couldn't help but display his shock on his face.

"It's all yours, my boy," Kropp.

* * *

Boyd's next stop was Arch Lamp's livery. He saddled his appaloosa and rode out for some exercise. After a few miles, he stopped, tied up the horse, and tried his hand with his pistol. Three years on the chain-gang hadn't helped his draw — but his aim was still true. Hitting the four fist-sized stones he set up on a boulder took him five shots. He spent a while practicing with his pistol until he loaded his last 5 bullets from his gunbelt into the pistol's cylinder, leaving one open — the one on which his hammer rested. He decided to head back to town.

That night he visited the Mark Twain saloon on Polk for a little poker. Word was already around that he was back in town. Several people stopped by the table where he was playing. Although he declined offers of free drinks, he did shake hands with men who had sat on his jury during the trial and some others he had known around Jefferson.

The next day when Boyd strolled around town, he occasionally ran into a few people he knew or at least recognized. Some had been acquaintances, and a couple had done business with him in his old life in Jefferson. Everyone seemed to be pleased to see him, but no one tried to engage him in conversation. Boyd was fine with that.

* * *

At the end week, Boyd went to The Bale of Cotton. As soon as he walked in, he all but ran over Daisy Philpot, a brassy blonde, a 20-year-old prostitute. She had been the woman he had saved from being killed by shooting her pimp, Godfrey Mull. As Boyd remembered it, the nattily dressed man had just pistol-whipped his 5 foot 6 inch soiled dove across the face with his revolver in this very saloon.

Now, Daisy stepped back inside. The smiling brown-eyed young woman had prominent breasts she displayed as much as possible.

Boyd stepped in, cleared the doorway, and removed his hat.

"The hero of Jefferson," Daisy sneered.

"I bed your pardon?"

"Oh, I doubt that very much. You don't beg for anything. You simply do the right thing, and the world worships you."

"What are you talking about?" Boyd asked.

"I never asked you for your help, Mr. Hero. Did you ever realize that?"

Boyd noticed that Daisy's left cheekbone was slightly caved in. Although she tried to hide it with makeup, the result was still evident. Boyd knew this was from the barrel of her pimp's shorten pistol.

"I can take care of myself, you ass!" she all but shouted at Boyd.

The saloon quietened as everyone in the place listened to the two figures by the door.

"You were on the floor — bleeding — unconscious."

"I would have been okay! Back then, I had carried a knife in my dress!" she said, producing a shiny Derringer and pointing it at Boyd's face.

"Mull had cocked his pistol and looked to me like he was going to shoot you."

"Like this," Daisy asked, pulling back the hammer on her weapon.

"Pretty much," Boyd said calmly.

"I needed to be taught a lesson! I'd been acting up all day! I do that sometimes! He was doin' what needed to be done."

After a moment of thought, Boyd said, "Is it possible that if I hadn't done what I did — you'd be dead right now? I thought I was doin' it for you."

Taken aback, Daisy said, "You sure as hell didn't do it for Godfrey."

"I agree. Any man who beats a woman deserves killin'." Boyd said nothing more for a bit as the two stood facing each other. Reluctantly, Boyd broke the silence saying, "Well, I guess I'm very sorry for stepping in," Boyd said. "It cost me 3 years of my life."

"It cost Godfrey his whole life! Hardly a fair trade." Daisy slipped her little pistol back into the folds of her dress.

"Maybe you'd be happier dead."

"Sometimes, I think I just might," Daisy said and pushed her way out of the saloon.

Dumbfounded, Boyd watched her go. He turned back to the room, and conversations picked up instantly.

"A beer, Boyd?" Layman Haverstick asked from behind the bar.

"Yeah," was all Boyd said.

"I can make it whiskey if you like."

"Beer is fine," Boyd said, stepping up to the end of the bar.

CHAPTER 5

After Boyd's first swallow of beer, Layman Haverstick flipped his bar towel over his shoulder as he leaned on the bar.

"I had no idea she felt that way," Boyd said. "She never spoke at my trial."

"Daisy has always been contrary. That night wasn't the first time Mull had slapped her around in public. It was the first time he'd clubbed her with his gun. Still, Daisy's lucky to be alive. She hasn't figured that out yet."

"Is she still working?"

"She is. For Vander Osby. He runs a string of girls, and she helps keep them in line. She was in here tonight — checking on Blossom and Manerva," he motioned with his head at two girls drinking with cowboys and drummers at different tables.

There was something in the way his partner had relayed this information that struck Boyd. As he looked back at Layman, Boyd said, "What is the rest of it?"

It took Layman a moment to wipe his mouth with his bar towel before he could bring himself to say, "I've — I've — uh — I've rented out the rooms to Osby. All of them. That's were her girls do their business. It's the same arrangement he has with other saloons."

THE HUSSY AND THE HARDCASE

"That ends tonight. Right now."

"Wait a minute, Boyd, this is not your decision to —."

"How much of this bar do you own, Layman?"

Boyd's partner took a moment before he could say, "Forty-nine percent."

"And who owns the majority?"

Layman snorted and said, "You do."

"Right now. Get them out. This is a saloon — a high-class saloon. It's not a whore house that sells drinks."

Layman made a twisted face, tossed the bar towel over his other shoulder, and walked off to do what Boyd had instructed.

As Boyd watched his partner go, he heard a chair crashed to the floor at the saloon's rear. A scruffy stevedore jumped to his feet and cleared his jacket away from the pistol in his belt.

"Those are the cards I had in my hand!" the belligerent man bellowed.

Sitting across from the raging man was Sheriff Corwin Danforth. He stayed in his chair and calmly said, "While the rest of the room was watching the scene at the front door, you produced another card from your sleeve."

"I don't care if you are the Sheriff, old man," the sinewy roustabout hollered. "Get to your feet and draw! Nobody calls me a cheat!"

"You mean nobody's called you on it before? That's funny. You're not very good at it."

Danforth got up slowly as the rest of the men at the table moved back.

"This isn't worth dying for," the Sheriff said evenly.

"Remember that as you're falling down!"

"You can't outdraw both of us," Boyd said, making his way across the room to the table.

"I don't know who you are, mister," the man said, glancing at the approaching image of a man in a suit was stepping in the confrontation direction. "Stay the hell out of this!"

"I'm his new deputy," Boyd discovered himself saying.

"What?" the confused riverboat worker said, turning back to the

Sheriff and not taking his eyes off of Danforth. "Draw old man! Or I'll kill you where you stand!"

"You draw on him, and you draw on me," Boyd stopped eight feet away.

Another roustabout got to his feet at a nearby table and put his right hand over the pistol in his belt. "I'm backing Rocky's play," he said.

"Good," Boyd said. "This is going to be exciting. You two are going to die, but it will be a thrill for everybody else." To Danforth, Boyd said, "Which one do you want?"

"I'll take the ugly one here who tried to cheat everybody at the table."

"Let's do it this way," Boyd said after a second, "the first one to pull gets to be the first one to die."

The cheater jerked his pistol, and Boyd fired before the stevedore got the barrel of his weapon up to the table's edge. Boyd's shot pierced the man's chest. The other riverboatman went for his pistol. Boyd fanned his hammer and shot the second man before the Sheriff got off his first shot and hit the already slumping cheater. The sound was like a rat-a-tat-tat. The last tat was from the Sheriff's pistol.

Both laborers dropped to the floor without firing a single round.

"You are slowing down," Boyd said to the Sheriff.

"I told you so," Danforth said, holstering his revolver.

"Nobody likes to hear that," Boyd said, shucking two empty shells and reloading his pistol.

Boyd directed some men to drag the two bodies out and put them in the brick street. Sheriff Danforth sent another to get the undertaker.

While this was going on, Layman was getting Blossom and Manerva out the door. The two whores didn't need much convincing to be on their way. They didn't believe the bartender when he told them not to come back.

"We don't work for you, Layman, the older of the two said. "Vander Osby will have something to say about this."

"When he does, have him say it to Boyd Spanner," Layman said as he left the two on the boardwalk and held the door for the men hauling the bodies to the street.

"Oh, he will," the older hooker said. "He will."

CHAPTER 6

Back in the Sheriff's office, cleaning their weapons, the Sheriff said, "I guess you've made up your mind."

"Seems like it," Boyd grudgingly admitted.

"I like the idea of your being my deputy."

"That came off the top of my head. I need to learn to keep my mouth shut."

"You kept the top of my head from being shot off. But if you are my deputy, you can follow me around and get a handle on the job."

"Don't you have other deputies?"

"One. Over East of here in Gray. Near Caddo Lake. Wheaton Falby helps with tax collections, but he's older than me. He doesn't even carry a pistol. He has a double-barrel .12 gauge he lugs with him. But he was a sergeant major back in the war — he doesn't put up with guff from anyone."

"And he's not interested in being Sheriff?"

"He's not leaving Grey. Plans to be buried on what's left of the family plantation there."

"Collecting taxes?"

"Oh, yeah, that's part of the job."

Marion County had been split off from Cass county to its North by before the war and Reconstruction. It was named after Revolutionary War hero Francis Marion, known as The Swamp Fox. It wasn't a populated part of East Texas. What wasn't piny woods was plantations, swamps, and bayous. Gray was only one of the other towns in the county. It was further East. Kellyville and Lasseter were West while Jefferson was in the center.

The two men worked on their sidearms in silence for a few minutes.

When Boyd was finished, he looked at Corwin Danforth a moment before saying, "I guess you need to swear me in and give me a badge."

The Sheriff opened the bottom drawer of his desk. He pulled out a deputy badge. From his bookshelf, Corwin Danforth picked up his Bible. He put the book on the desk and raised his right hand. Boyd placed his left hand on the Bible and raised his hand. He recited the oath word for words after Sheriff's Danforth. When the oath was sworn, Danforth pinned the badge on Boyd's coat.

"How does that feel?"

Boyd looked down at the piece of metal on his chest.

"Odd. Better than a hole, I guess. But it's strange. Kind of like my first day in prison."

"Well, you lived through that, hopefully, you'll live through this."

A horse was heard riding up to the office in a hurry. The rider stepped into the lamplight on the boardwalk as he tied up his mount.

Sheriff Danforth said, "Remember my telling you about Vander Osby?"

Boyd reholstered his pistol. He had one hip on the Sheriff's desk and was whipping his hands when the door banged open.

A man in brown and white plaid pants, coat and vest, shoved his way into the office. The vest strained to contain his belly, but his bulbous nose dominated his veined face. He stopped just inside the door frame and put his puffy hands on his hips.

"You killed two of my men," he announced.

"They were warned," Sheriff Danforth said. "You might say they killed themselves. In fact, that may be the way I write it up in my report."

Vander Osby turned to Boyd.

"I heard you were back, Boyd," he snarled. "And back to what you do best? Killing people."

"I can put you on a waiting list if you'd like, Vander."

The blustering man blanched and swallowed.

"And what's this about kicking my girls out of your saloon?"

"You said it. I'm the majority owner of The Bale. We don't deal in whores. I doubt it will do any damage to your and Daisy's business."

"It ain't Daisy's business."

"I didn't really think so," Boyd said. "I was being generous. Won't make that mistake again."

"But you will make a mistake — of some kind. And I'll see you get back to prison when you do."

"Boyd's my deputy now," the Sheriff said, coming around the desk loading his pistol. "Unless I say so, anything he does is within the law."

"Well, then I will have to run for the Sheriff's office."

"We thought you had already made up your mind to do just that, Vander. Only difference now is that people will have a choice."

"A convict. A known killer!"

"At least he's not a carpetbagger."

Those words angered Vander more than anything.

"You rebs lost the war. When are you going to get that through your thick heads?"

"We acknowledged that," Boyd said, getting to his feet. "But one thing Texas never needed was Reconstruction — and carpetbaggers was another."

"Reconstruction ain't over until I say it is! We still have a company of soldiers out at Fort Jefferson. And Col. Pardee sees things my way."

"You'd best think about that, Vander," Sheriff Danforth said. "Your soldier support won't be here forever. What will you do when you have no authority or anything to back it up? There are a lot of people in this town who'd like to see you wake up dead some morning. The only thing that keeps you alive is the law — not the Army. You best not mess with it."

Vander Osby stomped out the door slamming it behind him.

Boyd and Danforth listened as Vander's saddle strain as the man heaved himself on his horse and raced away.

"He's not just hot air," the Sheriff said.

"He's at least that — always has been."

"He is right about having Pardee behind him."

Col. L. Lavern Pardee was the commanding officer of Fort Jefferson. He'd been a lite colonel of supply during the war. He got a raise in rank by taking this reparation's post in the flimsy fort they build South of the town. Fort Jefferson wasn't much of a fortress, but it did make its presence known in East Texas. No war damage needed Reconstruction anywhere in Texas — only the social order — the loyalty and submission of the defeated Texans in this former thriving river port that was his mission. In that vein, carpetbagger, and marauding gangs of freed blacks fought with The Knights of the Rising Sun — the local variation of the KKK.

"What does that mean to us?"

"Not much. The law is the law — straight and simple. Both the scalawags and the klan try to twist things. We don't play that game."

CHAPTER 7

Among the other businesses, Vander Osby was involved in was his smuggling enterprise. Using the roustabouts on the docks, and teamsters driving wagons down the Jefferson Road, from North of Dallas to the Caddo Lake, Vander operated a criminal enterprise of stolen sugar, salt, tobacco, liquor, gold and silver to Jefferson. The goods came from gangs of scallywags, including discharged soldiers from both sides of the war who raided above and East of Dallas. Their collected goods were picked up South side of the upper CaddoLlake by riverboat headed East to the Mississippi.

Osby conducted his planning session in different places, preferring abandoned farms, ranches, and plantations in the area. Second in command of the operation was a freeman named Percy Early. Like his boss, Early wore a bowler hat and suit. But he liked flashy stickpins for his ties and a heavier than normal gold chain for this pocket watch. Early was not intimidating himself, standing a little over 5 feet 7 inches. However, he always surrounded himself with four other freedmen toughs who were hard-drinking, hard-fighting, working men who disliked baths but loved sleeveless shirts to display their muscles.

Two nights after his confrontation with Boyd and Danforth, Osby, Early, and their three-man bodyguard, rode through the moonlight to a barn on the abandoned Whitington plantation. This was pay off meeting with Osby's teamsters and move goods across the lake. Osby had demanded that his men row boats across Caddo Lake to meet up with outgoing paddle wheelers on the South side of the lake.

As the five men drew up in front of the barn, a dozen men in white sheet robes and hoods with only eye holes stepped out of the darkness.

"What —?" was all Osby could say before the armed men encircled Osby's group.

"This is the end of the line for you, Vander Osby!" the leader called out. This man had a rising red sun with streaking rays embroidered into the front of his robe and held a pistol in his hand. "We already have your boat and your men."

"Is that you, Norris?" Osby asked.

"You'll never know," the man said cocking his pistol.

"Well, let me say this —," Osby said in a loud voice. That was a signal for his men to all draw and fire.

The three bodyguards who held Henry rifles on their knees swung their weapons to their sides and fired. Vander and Percy Early pulled pistols and began firing at the men closest to them. Three robed men dropped to the ground, and the rest scattered as the smuggler continued their assault. One of the bodyguards was struck in the forearm, and the gunfight raged.

Vander was the first to wheel around and race away. Early and the other bodyguards were quickly behind him. They galloped up the road down which they'd come and were soon lost in the shadows.

A couple of miles away, Early pulled up as the wounded bodyguard slumped over his saddle horn. Early got down and caught the man before he could fall out of the saddle.

Vander realized he was alone, and he slowed to a stop.

"What th' hell's goin' on back there,?" he called.

"Bobby was shot!" Early yelled back.

Vander returned to the group. From the look of the injured freedman, the bullet that hit him tore off a good chunk of meat from the right forearm. He'd never been a good bodyguard again.

"Stop the bleedin'," Vander ordered. "Wrap it up tight, and we'll get him to a doctor."

The other men ripped up their dirty shirts into strips of cloth, and soon the man's arm was encased in rags collecting the blood.

"Don't anybody move!" The voice of Boyd Spanner came out of the dark.

"If you do, you die," Sheriff Danforth said from nearby. "And I know you, Vander. Shut up. You even say a word, and I'll plug you right through your pump where you sit. Everybody raise your hands."

The men did as they were told this time after a glance to Vander, who was already raising his hands.

Boyd moved into the moonlight, his .44 aimed at Vander Osby. The deputy pulled out the carpetbagger's pistol from his shoulder holster and yanked the man in the plaid suit out of his saddle. When Boyd had collected all the other weapons, Vander did speak.

"How'd you know where we were?"

"A little bird told me," Boyd said. To the injured man, he said, "Can you ride?"

"Yes, sir."

"Then, get to your feet."

"A little bird. Don't you mean a soiled dove? I'll whip that little bitch to within an inch of her life."

Boyd started to say, "You already have," but decided instead to say, "Daisy? Why in hell would she talk t' me?"

"Yeah," Vander said, sagging. "You did kill her pimp."

"She did manage to get another one, I hear."

"Now tell my deputy and me what happened." Sheriff Danforth said.

Vander stalled for a moment to think the matter over and then said, "I was going to meet with some associates. At the ol' Whitington plantation."

"Associates?" Danforth asked.

"You didn't even ask what happened?" Vander protested.

"Tell us," Boyd said.

"It was your damn klan. They tried to kill us all."

"Did you kill any of them?" the Sheriff asked.

"One or maybe two," Vander said.

"Then they'll hunt you down and hang you by morning. We'll jest let you go."

"You can't let them do that. They ambushed us! We were only defending ourselves."

The Sheriff thought the matter over and then said, "The only way I can help is to put you into protective custody."

"You mean to put us in jail?"

"It's either that or early morning swing on a short rope."

"All right. Do that. But you got to protect us."

"I'll do that until I get the whole story."

"It's exactly like I told you."

The Sheriff put his handcuffs away. The freedman helped the injured man to his saddle horn.

"Mount up," Danforth said. "Boyd, bring up the rear and make sure we're not followed."

CHAPTER 8

Doctor Emmet Askew was the youngest physician in town. At 35, however, he had gained a lifetime of experience during his two years in the war. His family had sent him to Scotland for medical school in 1858. Even though he wanted to return home at the beginning of the war, his parents demanded that he stay and become the best doctor he could. Once he had his degree in hand, he sailed back to New Orleans. He had to sneak past Union lines to get to Confederate forces to join the struggle and began that day doing battlefield surgery.

Following the war, Emmet Askew took a full year to make it back to Jefferson, where his parents lived. He opened a practice and proved to be every bit a knowledgeable and compassionate doctor he had hoped to be. Being the newest doctor in town, his early patients were often those on the lower end of the social scale, and he became the primary physician for the soiled doves of town.

He had seen women, girls really, beaten, cut, abused, and even shot in the course of his civilian practice. The damage done to Daisy Philpot amazed even him. She had been horsewhipped, and her skin laid open by the beating she had taken when he was called to The Dove's Roost, one of Vander Osby's bordellos. The short, brassy blonde, had lashes over every part of her body. Holding her hand was another dove, Juana Bell Irvin. This one was mulatto. She'd been the one who had summoned Boyd and hurried back to the doctor's office to be with her friend. Juana Bell had helped as well as any nurse Dr. Askew had ever worked with.

Daisy was awake and screaming in pain, but refused the tincture of opium, known as Laudanum, the Doctor had offered. Not until she talked to Boyd Spanner, she demanded. She cried and twisted, unable to find a comfortable way to lie until the deputy entered the room.

Boyd went to Daisy's side but saw the blood seeping through the sheet the doctor and his helper had draped over her. She grabbed his hand and said, "I'm sorry, Boyd. I was wrong about what I said to you. I was also wrong about Godfrey. He would have killed me — and you saved my miserable life."

"Forget that," Boyd said. "Who did this to you?"

"Vander Osby," she said through gritted teeth. "He's gone to get his payoff from his smuggling. He went to the Whitington plantation. Please get him, Boyd? Please," she pleaded grasping for the spoon full of unconsciousness the doctor held. She gulped it down and accepted a drink of water. A moment later, after two more painful screams, she relaxed and was asleep. Juana Bell stroked her friend's limp hand.

* * *

When Sheriff Danforth and Boyd returned to town with Osby and his crew, the Sheriff put the freedman into a cell and put Vander in a cell by himself.

"Aren't you going to lock these cell doors?" Vander demanded when Sheriff Danforth walked back to his office.

"I can," the Sheriff said. "But they can shoot you through the bars. Do you want to be in here locked up if they get past Boyd and me?"

"No," was all Vander could say as he flopped on the bed in his cell.

Boyd left the jail and took all the horses to the livery before he made his way to the Dove's Roost to fetch Dr. Askew. Daisy had been moved to the doctor's office and was sleeping when Boyd arrived. Dr. Askew said he had done all that could be done and believed she would recover. The other prostitute who had helped him with Daisy said she would stay and watch over her friend while the doctor went with Boyd.

The wounded freedman was patched up at the jail, and his forearm wrapped in fresh, clean bandages. Back out in the office before he left, Dr. Askew told the Sheriff and Boyd that if, not just the one who was hurt but his companions, too, had best leave Jefferson as soon as they could if they liked living.

"Exactly what Sheriff Danforth told them," Boyd said. "We're only keeping them here in case the Knights of the Rising Sun decide to find them again tonight."

"I told the one that was shot to keep his arm clean — but I, from the smell of all of them, I doubt any of them can do that. If not, gangrene is going to set in, and that will kill him."

"Thanks, Doc," Sheriff Danforth. "Send me the bill, and I'll see the county pays it."

"Shouldn't that be for Vander Osby to pay?"

"You've worked on his girls before — how good is he as paying up?"

"Good point, Sheriff. I'll send the bill to you."

* * *

A half-hour after Dr. Askew had gone, a thunder of hooves rushed out of the night and pulled up in front of the jail.

"Here they are," Danforth said, getting to his feet from behind his desk and taking two Greener shotguns down from the gun rack. He tossed one to Boyd.

In fact, the two double-barreled .12 gauge coach guns were made by Remington. In those days, it was common practice to refer to such weapons as "cut-down" or Greener shotguns because of the Greener full chokes common to these close-range guns.

Both the Sheriff and Boyd stuffed their pockets with extra double-ought buck-shot shells. Boyd opened the door, and both men stepped out under the boardwalk overhang.

In front of them were a gaggle of white-robed and hooded riders. Four men carried flaming torches. Their leader, the one with the red embroidered emblem on his robe, said, "We want Vander Osby, Percy Early, and those other three black boys!"

"They're in protective custody," Sheriff Danforth said, pulling back both hammers of his shotgun as Boyd did the same thing.

"You ready to die for that trash?" the leader growled.

"If that's what it takes, Norris Ballard, but you and a couple of your friends are going to go with us," Danforth said. Leaning his head slightly toward Boyd, the Sheriff said, "That's Norris Ballard."

Boyd aimed his double barrel in the leader's direction.

"We can't both miss," Boyd said.

One of the riders eased away from the group to the side of the jail, but the Sheriff saw him move.

"You can't prove who any of us are," another rider said.

"Oh, I know you, too, Gaston Cafrey," Danforth said.

"One of them is trying to get behind the jail," Boyd said to the Sheriff.

"I saw him. Can you handle this bunch by yourself?"

"I might have to kill a few, but I'll manage."

Danforth stepped back, opened the door, and went inside the jail just as a shot rang out from behind the building. Then two more shots were heard.

Boyd took the occasion to swing his shotgun up and fire a shot that blew out one of the torches and exploded flames all around. The hooded riders had to grab their reins to control their mounts.

Another shot was heard inside the jail. This was another shotgun blast.

"I've still got one more barrel itching to go!" Boyd said to Norris Ballard. "You see what this thing can do. You want to taste it?"

The rider behind the building was heard riding away.

"We'll remember you, Boyd Spanner!"

"And I'll remember you too, Ballard. And you Cafrey. And the one with the chip out of his right boot heel — and you with the red ring on — as well as all your horses! Now get before you get more lead than you can stomach!"

The gang pulled back, turned, and rode away.

CHAPTER 9

Boyd stood on the jail boardwalk as the Knights Of The Rising Sun left. He replaced the spent shell in his Greener but stood his ground for several more minutes. He did call into the jail, "Sheriff, are you okay?"

"I'm good," came the reply, "but Vander has been shot."

When Boyd finally returned to the jail, the laid his shotgun across the desk before going back to the cell area.

Vander Osby was on the floor with a belt being pulled tightly around his upper right leg. The bottom of the man's plaid pants were blood soaked.

"Want me to go get a doctor?" Boyd asked after checking to insure the freedmen were unhurt.

"Yeah," Sheriff Danforth said. "Doctor Askew's office is the nearest."

Boyd turned to go when Vander called out, "I don't want that whore doctor! Get me Doc Givens!"

"Givens," Boyd said as he left.

Sheriff Danforth stayed with Vander Osby but talked over his shoulder to the men in the other cells.

"Those who wanted to hang you all are gone. There's never going to be a better time for you boys to make tracks."

The men talked it over and decided to follow the Sheriff's advice. The last one paused at the door to Vander's cell and said, "We's goin' t' Mt. Vernon or ma'be Greensville."

"Good," Vander struggled to say. "Don't come back here."

Then the men peered out the door of the Sheriff's Office and ran into the dark.

* * *

Doctor Julius Givens was a man whose body didn't wear clothes well. He was in his early 50s and had a full beard like many Confederate generals during the war. His was laced with white, and the dark brown was fading. He wore a top hat that covered a bald head.

He took over for Sheriff Danforth to cut away the bloody material of Vander's leg. The Sheriff washed his hands at a water pump in front of the jail before filling a pan and setting it on the stove as the doctor ordered.

Boyd was in the office cleaning his shotgun. The Sheriff began to do the same with his weapon.

"I saw the cell window. You got off one shot I saw."

"But whoever was out there took three shots at Vander."

"Did you hit him?"

"Couldn't tell. All I know is that he rode off. I heard you fire once. I thought we were going to be in trouble."

"I blew one of the torches out they were carrying. It made such a sight I don't think any in that mob wanted to try the other barrel."

"Good thinkin'." After a few more cleaning moments, the Sheriff said, "Tomorrow we'll need to go out to the Whitington place. There could be some bodies there, although I doubt it. I'll bet good money there's blood on the ground. Doesn't help us much, but it will back up Vander's story of self-defense."

"Did you ever doubt it?"

"Nope. Hell, for a nickel, I'd shoot the som-bitch. Who, except those on his payroll, wouldn't."

"Water!" the doctor called from the cell.

"I'll get it," Boyd said, reloading his shotgun and returning it to the gun rack. He used his handkerchief to take hold of the pan of boiling water by two sides and take it to the cell.

Doctor Givens pulled the slug out of Vander's calf as the injured man screamed. The slug was dropped into a smaller pan on the bed with a clink. The doctor extracted a bottle of liquid from his medical bag, which he poured on Vander's leg. Vander passed out. Next, he took a cloth he soaked in hot water Boyd had brought and cleaned the wound.

"Bring a lamp over here," Givens ordered.

Boyd got the lamp on the wall across from the cells and brought it back. He held it as the physician threaded a needle and took four stitches to close the wound. After that, Givens pulled three rolled up bandages and wrapped them around Vander's leg.

When he was finished, he washed his hands in the now warm water.

"I'm going to leave him here for tonight," the doctor said. "I'll bring him a crutch tomorrow and help him back to my office."

Boyd returned the lamp to the wall.

"Anything the Sheriff or I can do for him tonight?"

"You might try seeing that nobody else shoots him," Givens grumbled as the got up and repacked his equipment. "It's a hell of a thing — a man getting shot while he's in custody."

"You might tell that to the boys down at the Kahn Hotel," Sheriff said from the office doorway.

Givens wants to say something more, but either good sense or anger kept his mouth shut. He pushed his way past Sheriff Danforth and left the jail.

"You think they'll try it again," Boyd asked.

"Doubt it. But I'll prop a chair against the wall here just in case."

"Whatever you say."

"You did good tonight, Boyd. Just like I always thought you would. Go get yourself some rest, and I'll see you tomorrow."

* * *

Boyd and Sheriff Danforth stopped at The Bale of Cotton before heading out to the old Whitington plantation. Bartender and co-owner Layman Haverstick was helping clean up. When Boyd and the sheriff stepped in, Layman said, "Heard about last night. Glad I wasn't there."

"Layman, I want to change some things. Move the pool tables over to the side and take out the first room on both sides downstairs. I want to build a stage there — bring in some singers, dancers, maybe some actors from time to time. Clean out all the other rooms, get new furniture, wallpaper, a rug runner up the stairs, and a rug downstairs and downstairs hallways. This is not a whore house anymore. It's a saloon — a high-class saloon — with a few rooms to rent."

"Where's the money coming from for all this?" Layman protested.

"I'll cover it. Don't worry about that. Repaint the walls in here, get new felt for the tables. I want the riff-raff to see when they step in the door that this is not their kind of place."

"Well, it's your money."

"It sure is."

**

The big house at the former plantation had been burned to the ground. Only the barn and the outbuildings were still standing, although some were beginning to suffer from time and weather.

As expected, no bodies were found, but bloodstains in the dirt were evident in several places. The trail of horses led to the North. Boyd and the Sheriff followed it back to town, where the hoof prints were lost on Jefferson's bricked streets.

"About what I expected," Danforth said when he and Boyd turned their horse into Arch Lamp's livery.

"Did you have many lathered horses come in last night — late?" the Sheriff asked Arch.

"Can't say I did."

"Can't or won't," Boyd asked.

"I'm no fan of the klan, and they don't control me," he barked at Boyd.

"Most of these men would keep their horses at home," Danforth said.

"I'll recognize some of the horses that were out in front of the jail last night," Boyd said.

"I wouldn't expect to see any of those animals around anytime soon. My guess is that many will be sold out of town pretty soon."

"So, this is a dead end."

"For the moment."

A bulky man wearing a badge, accompanied by two rifle carrying men, walked into the livery. This was Town Marshal Raymond Roggy. The thick-necked 32-year-old had fancy sideburns that swept up into a thick mustache and light blue eyes.

"Sheriff Corwin Danforth, you're under arrest for the attempted murder of Vander Osby — in your own jail."

CHAPTER 10

Town Marshal Raymond Roggy was a carpetbagger political appointee. The best thing about him was that he was lazy. The town knew he existed and had both an office and a couple of deputies. To most people, Roggy was the best kind of carpetbagger if they had to have carpetbaggers at all. No one ever saw any of the trio unless they were out drinking or whoring. He hadn't even come to investigate the two men Boyd, and Sheriff Danforth had killed in the Bale of Cotton shootout.

"Come on," he said in is quick Yankee accent. "I'll need your pistol as evidence. I'm sure Judge Waberton will let you out on your own recognizance."

"Who says I shot Vander?" Sheriff Danforth asked his anger creeping up his neck.

"The victim. Doctor Givens has the bullet."

"Bullet? I never fired my pistol. I shot at somebody through the window with my Greener.'

"That's none of my affair," Roggy said. A warrant was issued, and I'm here to enforce it."

Sheriff Danforth unbuckled his gunbelt and handed it over.

"Is that bastard Hamlin Cranford still the District Attorney?" Boyd asked as he forced himself not to pull on the Marshal and his deputies.

"He is. He wrote out the warrant. And he speaks kindly of you, too, Boyd," the Marshal said.

"This is more horseshit than Arch has to deal within a month," the Sheriff said.

Boyd took the belt and followed the trio as they paraded Danforth up Polk Steet.

* * *

Pompous carpetbagger Judge Collie Waberton sat high behind his desk, awaiting town Marshal Roggy and his deputies to bring in Sheriff Danforth. District Attorney Hamlin Cranford sat at the prosecution table wearing a stiff white collar and a spotless suit. He had thinning hair, bushy eyebrows, and beady eyes.

The Judge smoked a long cigar as he lounged in his judicial robe. He sat up when Boyd entered after the expected party.

"Boyd Spanner, what are you doing here?" District Attorney Cranford asked.

"I came to see an honest judge at work."

"Well, I'll have none of your sarcasm in this court," Judge Waberton said.

"Of course not," Boyd said. "I wouldn't want to spoil the mood."

"Another word out of you, and I'm sure the judge will hold you in contempt," Cranford said.

Boyd just smiled, knowing he had done his work.

The District Attorney was on his feet and lifted an official document the began speaking. "You, Sheriff Corwin Danforth, are charged with the attempted murder of Vander Osby while holding him in protective custody."

"And how did I do that, Hamlin?" the Sheriff asked the DA. "I forget."

"You shot him through the bars while a crowd of klansmen waited outside to cover for you."

"That's not how I remember it."

"Unfortunately, that's the way Mr. Osby remembers it."

"I don't see my accuser anywhere," the Sheriff said, looking around the empty courtroom.

"You will during the trial. At the moment, Mr. Osby in under Doctor Givens's care."

"And the other four witnesses? The freedman."

"What freedmen?" the attorney asked. "I don't know anything about any freedmen."

"The ones in the other two cells?"

"No one else seems to know about them."

"I do," Boyd said.

"You've been warned once, Mr. Spanner."

"Didn't Doc Givens tell you about them?" Danforth asked.

"He never said a word to me," Marshal Raymond Roggy said.

"How about Doctor Askew?"

"Askew? What's he got to do with it?" the Marshal insisted.

"He was in the jail treating one of the wounded freedmen before the mob showed up."

"No one's said anything about him to me."

"You'll have your day in court to prove otherwise," Judge Waberton said. "A week from today."

"I week?"

"This court believes in swift justice."

Sheriff Danforth forced himself to remain silent.

The Judge went on, "But for the moment you have been officially charged. How do you plead?"

"Since I didn't do it, I'm going to pick, 'Not Guilty.'"

"So entered into the record," the Judge said, scribbling a note on a tablet in front of him. "And if I have your word you won't try to leave the jurisdiction of this court, I will release you on your own recognizance."

"You have my word," Danforth said, slowly trying to control his temper.

* * *

"I should have kept my mouth shut," the Sheriff said as he and Boyd walked back to the jail.

"You said what you had to."

"I didn't have to say anything about Dr. Askew. His life is now in danger."

"Why don't I go check on him?" Boyd asked. "I'll tell him to be on his guard."

"Good idea. I'd sure hate for something to happen to that young man. He doesn't have a great reputation in town because he looks after the doves — but he's a fine doctor."

"Tell you what, I can hang around his office the next couple of days if you think I should," Boyd said.

"You'd do more good there than with me. I doubt anything is going come of our night riding adventure."

"You need to see about getting you a good lawyer."

"How about Less Barbur?"

"He got me 3 years on the chain gang."

"But he almost got you off. If it hadn't of been for Judge Tewilliker …"

"You're right. And I don't blame Less. I'm going by his office. I'll send him over to the jail to see you."

"Thanks, Boyd."

"You'll know where to find me," Boyd said, walking away.

CHAPTER 11

"I heard. Bad news travels faster than a stampede," Doctor Emmet Askew said. The physician was in his shirt-sleeves, his tie loosened, and he spoke to Boyd at the front door of his front office on Line Street. "Where are the four in the other cell?" he asked.

"They took your advice and left town."

"Including the one I patched up?"

"Of course."

"I shouldn't have said anything."

"No, you most likely saved their lives."

"And put Sheriff Danforth's neck in a noose?"

"We'll see. I think Less Barbur Is going to represent."

"Come in, Boyd. Can I get you some coffee?" the doctor asked, opening the door and motioning the deputy in.

"I can always take a cup," Boyd removed his hat as he stepped in and closed the door behind him. While the doctor poured two cups and Boyd took a seat near the physician's roll top desk.

"The reason I'm here is that you were there that night and saw those four. Now that they're gone, Vander will claim they were never there."

"But you saw them, Boyd? You can testify to that."

"Yes, but I'm an ex-con. Who'd believe me?"

"Most of the people in this town, that's who."

"We'll see. But you're also in danger. If something were to happen to you — by accident, let's say — and you weren't there to also say those men were there — well, it would be hard to prove."

The doctor's face went slack.

"You think someone wants me killed?"

"Sheriff Danforth thinks, too."

"You're to be my baby sitter?"

"How about 'bodyguard.'"

"Six of one, half dozen of the other."

"Doc, we'd rather you keep breathing. Do you think you can put up with me for a week or so?"

"How long?"

"The trial is set for next week. That's a lot of opportunities for accidents."

The young physician sagged in his chair and nodded his head.

"You have to understand, most of my business is not here. I go where people are hurt, children have done something stupid — or one of the town's doves needs my attention."

"I'll go with you, Doc — if you'll let me."

"I don't mind — but people may want to see me in private."

"Got it. I can step outside or take a stroll around the house."

"Then I think we can work this out."

* * *

"They've set you up," attorney Less Barbur said, standing inside the cell where Vander Osby had been shot through the window. "Hamlin Cranford will tell the jury not to believe anything Boyd says because he just got out of prison. If those four men have left town, there's no way we'll ever find them and get them to testify."

"Are you sayin' I'm done?"

"No. But you need to know, it's going to be an uphill fight. Proving a negative is always harder than proving a positive. Like trying to prove God doesn't exist. There's too much evidence that He does.

"Now an attempted murder trial a week after the event is unheard of. It's a rush to judgment. And Judge Waberton is both a carpetbagger and he's in Vander Osby's pocket."

"I know," said the Sheriff. "I think the whole town knows Cranford and Marshal Roggy are, too. A stacked deck."

"We'll get a say in who sits on the jury."

"But can't he overrule the jury?"

"Oh, he could — but I have requested an Official Observer from the Texas Supreme Court to be present. And I've informed Judge Waberton of the fact. The observer will be present in the court but not identified. And, too, the carpetbaggers don't have the power or influence they used to. I'll do everything I can. There's more than one way to skin this cat.

"And one more thing — this could be a way of winning an election."

"I never even considered that. I'll do whatever you say, Less."

"First, tell me the whole story again — and don't leave anything out."

* * *

The second day Boyd spent with Doctor Askew, the physician stepped out of his backroom and spoke to his bodyguard.

"Boyd. Daisy would like to speak to you."

"Is she in her right mind? She wants to talk to me?"

"You'll see."

"If she wants to take another chunk out of my ass — I don't think I'm interested."

"I've given her something to ease the pain and to help her sleep. But go on in."

Boyd got up and thought for a second. He went to the front door and locked the door.

"Don't open this without my bein' in here," Boyd told the doctor.

Doctor Askew understood and nodded his head.

Boyd slowly stepped across the front office and went through the opened door to the two beds in the physician's back room.

Daisy was on the first bed, her arms outside the covers. The marks of the whipping from Vander Osby were very evident on the young woman's arms. Her face, minus the usual makeup, looked more innocent and even more youthful than Boyd had ever seen her.

To Boyd, Daisy had always seemed to be a flashy brassy blond with prominent breasts and a brash seductive attitude. The person he saw now lying in the bed had limp hair, red, closed eyes, and a sad expression.

"Daisy," Boyd said quietly.

She looked up at him slowly and said, "Sit down, Boyd."

Boyd looked around and found a straight-backed chair against the wall. He pulled it over beside the bed and sat.

"Thank you," she said softly. "You didn't have to come the night I called you for help."

"It was my job."

She almost laughed but couldn't.

"I know you better than you do yourself, Boyd."

"I doubt that."

"You are not the hardcase you think you are. You're no softy — but you're not the hardass you want everyone to believe."

Boyd had no response to this. No one had ever talked to him like this.

Daisy lifted her hand and reached out to touch Boyd's arm.

"The first time I ever saw you, I wanted you — but you didn't want me. That made me mad. I've been mad at you for a long time. Not anymore." She held his eyes with hers a moment before saying, "I'll never go back to whorin'. Not just because I can't — I don't want to anymore. And I want to thank you for that."

"I don't understand."

"I've always known Godfrey Mull was one day going to kill me. I'd made myself believe that's what I deserved. Even after you shot him. Even after you came back — and I had traded Godfrey for Vander. I had to almost be killed to learn I wanted to live — to be something more than I am." Tears were streaming down her cheeks as she squeezed his hand and said, "And I owe that to you, Boyd."

She closed her eyes, took a deep breath, and went to sleep.

Boyd sat there until her fingers dropped from his arm back to the bed. When he got to his feet, it was slowly. What if Daisy was right? What if he was more than they thought? What if Daisy could become something more?

CHAPTER 12

"Who was that?" Dr. Askew asked, closing the door to the backroom as Boyd relocked the front door and holstered his pistol.

"Some kid. Said a Mrs. Grover was about ready to deliver. I told him you were tied up with a patient here and couldn't come. He said he'd go see Dr. Givens."

Emmet Askew frowned at Boyd, and his eyes narrowed.

"What?" Boyd asked.

"Sharing night call is the only thing the other local doctors in town have allowed me to do as a part of the local medical community. Tonight was my night on. Once every 9 days."

"Do any of them ever miss a call?"

"Sure, but I'm still trying to prove myself."

"Not tonight. Do you even know a Mrs. Grover?"

"Yes. She's the wife of Alver Grover. Newspaperman. Started up a paper called The Gazette."

"Is there any reason to think another doctor in town couldn't handle this?"

"No." Then after a second, the Doctor added, "Unless it's a difficult delivery."

"That a specialty of yours?"

"It has come to be. Because of the girls I treat, I've come up against several strange deliveries. These girls don't want to get pregnant. How can they be sure who the father is? And several try ol' wives remedies for abortions. When these don't work, it complicates everything. Some of them have second thoughts and want to keep their babies — but they've already created problems. As it turns out, I've become an obstetrician-gynecologist — a delivery and a woman's doctor."

"I didn't know there were such things?"

"More in Europe than here — but things are changing."

Dr. Givens took the call Boyd had refused and drove his buggy out Line Street headed North for East Dixon. The newspaperman had chosen to build his clapboard house outside the current residential area. He was betting on Jefferson growing, and his home and property improving in value as the two enlarged.

Line Street was the line between two different visions of what became Jefferson. The Red River Raft, the monolithic logjam which made the Red River impassable, had begun to be attacked by Captian Henry Shreve. The 100-mile long collection tree trunks, branches, and full-grown trees were set for removal by a project of the U.S. Army Core of Engineers.

Captain Shreve made traffic possible up the Caddo Lake on the Big Cypress Bayou. Alan Urquhart established a river ferry to move people and cargo across the bayou upstream from the lake. The settlers heading into Texas made Urquhart's enterprise profitable. With the land grant he got in 1841, he envisioned a town along the bayou long before it was a navigable waterway.

Daniel Nelson Alley came from Virginia with his parents. They settled in what became Marian County. The family built a mill on one of the Big Cypress Bayou tributaries that became known as Alley Creek. Life grew up around the mill and became Alley's Mills. With a post office, Daniel Alley saw the possibilities of what Alan Urquhart had begun. He purchased what Urquhart called the Alley Addition. Alley had his own plans for a town and laid out streets. His goal was along the lines of the compass, North, South, East, and West. Urquhart streets were about a 45-degree angle to Alley's and ran Northwest to Southeast, Northeast to Southwest. "The Line" became where the two plans met, and streets either ended or began.

At night Line Street was dark and tree-lined. Even though Jefferson had created a gas plant and installed street lamps in the downtown area, the residential areas were still lightless. But Dr. Givens gelding knew to stay on whatever street or road the Doctor had directed him to.

Dr. Givens was yawning when the first shot tore through the buggy. Within the few moments that followed, slugs from both sides pierced the Doctor's arms, legs, back, chest, and head. The startled horse was also hit and was able to take only a few more steps before he dropped to the road.

Men ran away from their hiding places on both sides except for one. Percy Early, Vander Osby's second in command who hadn't fled with the others from the jail. He wore a bowler hat and reloaded his pistol as he walked up to buggy where the downed horse snorted in pain. His flashy stickpins sparkled in what little moonlight there was.

But he as he leaned over the side of the buggy and lifted the deadman's head, he swore. He dropped the man's head and ran away but paused and came back. He put a bullet in the suffering horse's head.

CHAPTER 13

Counting the new Jefferson Gazette, there were three newspapers in town. The other two were The Jeffersonian and the Jefferson Jimplecute — known as the "Jimp." Founded in 1848, The Jimplecute was the oldest of the three. The weekly one sheet had become a weekly 3-page publication. When it had changed hands for the third time, months before Boyd killed pimp Godfrey Mull, Boyd had become a 15 percent investor in the paper. He had been on a winning streak and used some of the money to become a silent partner in the paper. He also pledged to never offer or request any input into the publication. It was a pledge he honored, and only he and the paper's owner knew he had put money into the venture.

The name of the Jimplecute was a subject of local legend and debate. One theory was the first publisher had spilled type font for the masthead and, in a rush, put them together in the unique word. Another claim was that the paper was named after a mythical creature with a dragon's mouth, the body of a mammoth armadillo, with a poison snake for a tail. It was a creation used to scare former slaves. Still, others said the word was an acronym to the paper's motto: "Joining Industry, Manufacturing, Planting, Labor, Energy, Capital (in) Unity Together Everlasting."

All three papers covered the murder of Dr. Givens. The Gazette came out on Mondays, The Jimplecute on Thursdays, and The Jeffersonian on Saturdays. At the physician's funeral, a crowd of locals, including Vander Osby and several freedmen, heard a sermon about the assassination's uselessness.

There were two other funerals earlier that week, prominent men who died unexpectedly. One had succumbed to a heart attack it was reported, and the other to a stroke. Sheriff Danforth and Deputy Boyd believed both men were killed at the Whitington plantation gunfight. But grieving family members denied such claims. Both men's causes of death were attested to by their family doctor. That physician, who signed both death certificates, was a known and ranking member of The Knights Of The Rising Sun. The brotherhood showed up in force at both burials.

The other big story was the trial of Sheriff Danforth, which was to begin the upcoming Monday.

* * *

City Marshal Roggy stood beside the bailiff and had one deputy at the end of the jury box and another beside the front door. Sheriff Danforth sat down at the defense table with his attorney, Less Barbur, after Judge Collie Waberton entered and took his seat. The Judge gaveled the court to order and had the bailiff, Morton Upton, read the charges. Upton was a former blacksmith and had one missing finger on his left hand.

Boyd sat behind Sheriff Danforth. Osby was on the front row behind the prosecution. The courtroom was full, and there were even people standing around the walls. One of them was Percy Early. He stood in a back corner, had a toothpick in his mouth, and stood with his arms crossed over his chest.

All the time Judge Waberton kept looking over the gallary of the courtroom hoping to pick out who the lawyer was from the Texas Supreme Court. The problem was Waberton didn't know everyone in and around Jefferson. There was one man in a fine suit the Judge spotted but he couldn't be sure this was who he was looking for. He was known as a Yankee carpetbagger and he didn't care to mingle with the common people of the town. Judge Waberton couldn't even put a name to either the pregnant woman or her husband sitting beside her. He only knew the man was the new Gazett newspaper publisher.

Vander Osby, limping and using a crutch, was the first witness District Attorney Hamlin Cranford called. He wore a different plaid suit but was the same overbearing carpetbagger the town had come to know. After being sworn in, Vander told his well-rehearsed tale of being shot by the Sheriff as a mob raided the jail. It was a vividly painted scene of a defenseless man wantonly gunned down by a lawman.

When the District Attorney yielded the witness to the defense, Less Barbur, stood and approached the witness box. The carrot red-haired, mustached, blue eyes and freckled-faced lawyer spoke in a clear voice.

"Why were you in Sheriff Danforth's jail, Mr. Osby?"

"He was supposedly protecting me from that mob outside."

"That mob was The Knights Of The Rising Sun, correct?"

"Yes."

"Why did you need protecting from these men?"

Vander tried to remember the answer he and Cranford had gone over.

"I had been attacked earlier that evening by them."

"Why did they attack you? Were you doing something illegal?"

"No!" Osby shouted. Then he remembered his instructions to remain calm. "I was meeting with associates. At the Whitington Plantation."

"As I remember, Union troops burned the Whitington Plantation toward the end of the recent conflict. Isn't that true?"

"Yes. Everybody knows that," Osby said, feeling in control again.

"What kind of meeting were you having at an abandoned plantation in the dark of night? Was this a board meeting? A business discussion. A meeting with investors? What kind of meeting was it?"

"Objection!" Hamlin Cranford demanded. "The nature of the witness's meeting is irrelevant. The fact that he was attacked is the issue."

"Your Honor," Less said to the Judge, "if the witness was in protective custody, it is significant to understand why that was needed."

"The witness has already stated he was meeting business associates," Judge Waberton said. "That a band of illegal marauders attacked him is all that the jury needs to know. Objection sustained. Move on, Mr. Barbur."

The defense attorney returned to the defense table. He consulted his notes and turned back to Vander.

"Mr. Osby, how many times did the Sheriff shoot you?"

"He tried three times but only hit me once."

"Three times. But he only hit you once."

"How big was the cell you were in?"

"I'd guess 10 by 12 feet."

"And where was the Sheriff when he fired his weapon at you?"

"Right outside the bars."

"So, no more than 10 or 11 feet away?"

"Yes."

"And it took him three shots to hit you?"

"I never said he was a good shot," Osby grinned.

This got a chuckle from some in the courtroom.

"After you were wounded — and the mob had left, did the Sheriff call you a doctor?"

"Yes, he did. I think the fact that the others saw what he had done made him finally do the right thing."

"Others? Were there others in the jail at the same time you were?"

"Uh — " Osby studdered, " — I mean the deputy. Boyd Spanner."

"There were no others in the jail? None of your other associates?"

"No."

"Which physician did the Sheriff go get for you?"

"He didn't go. He sent Boyd. He wanted to get the whore doctor, but I told him no, I wanted Dr. Givens."

"The same Dr. Julius Givens, who was murdered last week?"

"Yes."

"Do you have any idea why anyone would want Dr. Givens killed?"

"Objection," D.A. Cranford said. "Relevance?"

"Yes, Mr. Barbur," the Judge said. "That crime has nothing to do with the one this trial about. Move on."

Less Barbur sighed before asking, "Your testimony is you were alone in the jail under protective custody. That the Sheriff tried to kill you — shooting at you at about 10 feet and hitting you only once — in the leg. Then the Sheriff sent his deputy to secure a doctor to treat your wounds. Is that correct?"

"Exactly."

"Can you explain to the jury," Less Barbur asked, walking over and standing by the jury box, "why the Sheriff, who wanted to kill you, didn't shoot you when you were alone with him in the jail after the Deputy left?"

"I — I don't know."

"He could have, couldn't he? There was no one else to stop him?"

"Asked and answered," Hamlin Cranford objected.

"Move on, Mr. Barbur."

"No more questions, Your Honor."

CHAPTER 14

"Attorney Hamlin Cranford said, rising from the prosecution table with a sealed letter envelope in his hand. "At this time, the State would like to enter this envelope and its contents into evidence."

Cranford stepped up to the evidence table and read from the handwritten note on the envelope's front. "'Bullet removed in the Marion County jail this night from the leg of Mr. Vander Osby.' It is signed and dated by Dr. Julius Givens."

The District Attorney tore open one end of the envelope and tilted the paper package until a twisted lead chunk fell into the lawyer's hand. He held it between this thumb and forefinger as he displayed it to the Judge and the jury.

"Any objection from the defense?" Judge Waberton asked.

Less Barbur rose and crossed to the table. He examined the object saying, "It doesn't look like a bullet to me, Your Honor."

"The malleable lead is deformed because that's what happens when a slug impacts bone," Cranford explained.

"Is this all of it?" Barbur asked.

"According to Dr. Givens's note. He wrote nothing about there being any other fragments."

The defense attorney handed the bullet back to Cranford. "No objection," he said.

"Mark that as Prosecution Exhibit A," the Judge ordered. The bailiff made a note and placed the bullet and the envelope on the table.

Returning to his table, Hamlin Cranford said, "And this, Your Honor, we offer as our Exhibit B, the gunbelt and pistol of Sheriff Corwin Danforth."

"Are there any bullets missing from that weapon?" Less Barbur asked.

"One," Cranford answered.

"Is there a round missing, or is the hammer resting on an empty cylinder as is the common practice of men who carry revolvers?"

"Your Honor, this weapon was taken from the defendant the day after the victim was shot, the D.A. said. "Even if the empty chamber is vacant for the sake of safety as the defense contends, it is also very possible, if not, indeed, probable that any empty chambers would have been reloaded. Remember, the victim was fired at three times."

"Is this, or is it not the pistol of Sheriff Danforth?" Judge Waberton asked.

"It is," Less Burbar conceded.

"Then this pistol will be accepted as Prosecution Exhibit B."

The defense lawyer returned to his seat as the District Attorney faced the jury.

"At this time, the Prosecution planned to call Dr. Julius Givens to the stand to support and testify as to the wounds, the bullet, and the pistol used to shoot Mr. Osby."

"Objection," Less Burber said, rising to his feet. "Mr. Cranford knows he cannot describe what he hoped a missing witness might or might not have said. Nor can he testify himself to matters he discussed with the murdered physician. To do so would be to accept mere words supposedly heard by the Prosecutor from an absent witness say. Heresay testimony is not an accepted form of evidence."

"Sustained," the Judge ruled with a frown. "The District Attorney will restrict his remarks to facts in evidence alone."

Cranford did not take the rebuke well but said nothing for several moments until he returned to his table and shuffled through his notes and papers.

"Without the testimony of Dr. Givens," Cranford finally said, "the only other witness to the events is Deputy Boyd Spanner — and as a former convict, we do not put any faith in anything he might say."

"Objection," Burber said. "The State is disparaging a witness who has not been called."

It took a moment before Judge Waberton said with a scowl, "Sustained. This is unusual behavior for the District Attorney — but the Court does admonish Mr. Cranford to follow the proper rules of decorum and order in this trial."

"Yes," Your Honor," Cranford said without grace or acknowledgment of his conduct breach. "The Prosecution rests." Hamlin Cranford sat down.

"Defense, do you have a witness?" the Judge asked.

"Of course, Your Honor. I would like to call the accused, Marian County Sheriff Corwin Danforth to the stand."

The Sheriff was dressed in a clean shirt, polished boots, and his badge was gleaming as he took the stand. Danforth was sworn in and sat in the witness chair.

Less Burber approached and asked, "Sheriff Danforth, can you please give the jury your account of the events of the night in question?"

"We received word that Vander Osby and four other men were up to no good out on the Whitington Plantation Road. My deputy and I went out to investigate."

"Objection!" Harlin Cranfort shot to his feet. "What was the source of this 'word' the witness alludes to?"

"Your Honor, the Sheriff," Less said, "as a part of his work, has confidential sources that are not relevant to the issue at hand. The fact is, it doesn't matter who informed the Sheriff. He was following up on information he had been provided and was operating well within his capacity as the county's chief law enforcement officer."

The Judge had to hesitate before he ruled. He didn't like what the law required him to do. Thus he did it as quickly and simply as possible. "Objection denied. Move on, Mr. Burber."

Osby whispered to Hamlin Cranford, "It's that whore Daisy Philpot. I know it."

When Sheriff Danforth picked up his story, he said, "My deputy and I were about 3 quarters down the road toward the old plantation when we heard gunshots in the distance. Then we heard horses galloping in our direction. We decided to take cover on different sides of the road and see who was coming. It turned out to be Vander Osby, Percy Early, and three other freedmen. They stopped because one of the men had been wounded. Deputy Spanner and I got the drop on them when we stepped out of the shadows.

"It turned out that Vander and his — group — claimed to have been involved in an ambush with The Knights Of The Rising Sun at the Whitington Plantation. That's where one of them was shot. They knew the Knights would be after them and asked for our help. The only help we had to offer was to place them all in protective custody and put them in jail for the night. That's what we did — at least until the hooded mob showed up at the jail."

CHAPTER 15

Sheriff Corwin Danforth finished his story of the evening Vander Osby was shot in jail.

Running his hand through his thinning blond hair, Danforth said, "I saw one of the hooded riders slip beside the jail. I knew he could shoot through the barred windows, so I left Deputy Spanner by himself on the porch, and I hurried inside. Before I could get back to the cells, I heard two pistol shots. I came through the door to the cells as a third round was fired. I shot at someone in a hood outside the window on horseback."

"What weapon did you use when you took this shot, Sheriff?" Less Burber asked.

"My Greener. Twelve gauge street sweeper."

"Did you hit anyone?"

"Couldn't be sure — but I thought the bastard jerked. So I could have ..."

"The witness will not use profanity in this court!" Judge Waberton bellowed, banging his gavel.

"Beg your pardon, Judge," Danforth said as if he were sure such words were no stranger to the jurist.

"You were saying, Sheriff, I believe you might have at least wounded the assailant."

"Yes. Couldn't be sure, though. I do know that the next day Brit Jobe showed up at his store with an arm in a sling."

A man still wearing a sling a man stood up and shouted, "I fell off a ladder and hurt my shoulder. Doc Givens treated me."

"Objection!" District Attorney Cranford called out. "The witness is accusing an innocent man merely to support his testimony."

"Innocent," Sheriff Danforth said. "Let's take a look at that shoulder. I'll bet we'd see where some double ought buckshot has been dug out of it."

Judge Waberton slammed his gavel down several times. "Order in the court! I will have order, or I will clear this court!" Turning to the Sheriff, he said, "The witness will confine his remarks to facts in evidence! Objection sustained!" Waberton pounded his gavel once more.

"Let us continue," Less Burber said. "You used your shotgun to fire at someone who was using a pistol to shoot into the jail from the outside. Is that your testimony, Sheriff?"

"Yes," Danforth said after taking a breath and getting himself under control.

"What happened next?"

"I pulled open the cell door — which wasn't locked because they were in protective custody and not under arrest — and found Vander Osby shot in the leg."

"Did you try to help him?"

"Of course. I took off my belt and wrapped it around his leg above the wound to try and stop the bleeding."

"Were there any witnesses to this?" Less asked.

"Four. The freedmen who were riding with Osby when we took them into custody."

"What happened next?"

"I heard a shotgun blast from the front of the jail, and I was afraid Deputy Spanner had shot somebody in the mob."

"But he didn't?"

"No. Turns out, he just blew the hell — blew the daylights — out of one of their torches. That's all it took to get their attention. Soon after that, the mob broke up and rode off."

"Did Deputy Spanner come back inside the jail?"

"After a couple of minutes. He'd called out to make sure I was okay, but he stood his ground a minute or so to make sure the mob wasn't going to double back. Then he came in."

"And you sent him for a doctor?"

"Objection," Cranford said. "The defense attorney is leading the witness."

"Sustained," Judge Waberton ruled.

"I'll reword the question. When your deputy returned, what happened?"

"Boyd was the one who offered to get a doctor. I suggested Dr. Askew, but Vander demanded Doc Givens."

"Go on."

"Well, that's about it. Boyd went to get the doctor — oh, yes, the freedman decided they didn't want to be in custody anymore. They left. One of them said something about going to Mt. Vernon or Greensville. Vander told them not to come back."

"At anytime did you pull your pistol, Sheriff?"

"No, I didn't."

"Did you shoot Vander Osby in a cell in your jail?

"No. I tried to protect him."

"So, in summary, the only shot you fired was from your shotgun, which was at a hooded assailant outside the barred cell window?"

"That's right."

Less Burber walked back to the defense table, saying, "Your witness," to the District Attorney.

Hamlin Cranford rose and crossed to Sheriff Danforth. "Mr. Osby was in your jail, under your protection, and yet he was shot."

"Not by me," Danforth said. "Some joker in a hood outside the jail leaned in and tried to kill him. He did hit Vander once."

"But that wasn't you?"

"No, it was not."

"And these other prisoners who observed ..."

"They weren't prisoners. They were in protective custody — which they asked for."

"And they've all magically disappeared, now?"

"All but one."

"Who is that?" Cranford almost laughed.

"That fellow back there in the corner," the Sheriff pointed to Price Early.

All eyes went to Early, who started for the door, but Boyd got there first.

"Going somewhere?"

"Get out of my way, or I will kill ya' where ya' stand," Early threatened.

The sound of a pistol being cocked behind him cause Early to freeze. It was the bailiff, Morton Upton.

"Is this the man?" the bailiff Upton asked.

"That's him. Price Early."

Less Burber stood and said, "Your Honor, the defense would like to call Mr. Early as a witness."

The Judge looked at Cranford and at Osby, who was shaking his head. Then the Judge noticed the man in the nice suit who seemed to be paying more attention to the Judge than to the courtroom's commotion.

"Bring that man forward," the Judge order reluctantly.

"Better disarm him," Boyd said.

Bailiff Upton lifted Early's pistol from the freedman's holster while keeping his own gun trained on the man.

As Early turned toward the bailiff, Boyd reached down and pulled a knife out of the man's boot and offered it to the bailiff. The court officer waved Early forward and took the blade from Boyd.

CHAPTER 16

Judge Collie Waberton called a recess for lunch and had bailiff Morton Upton secure Price Early in a narrow detention cell on the courthouse's second floor.

In his chambers, the Judge waited for the District Attorney and Vander Osby.

While the Sheriff went to eat with attorney Less Burber, Boyd made his way with Dr. Askew to check on Daisy. As the Doctor unlocked his office door, he and Boyd heard singing.

"Down by yon flowery garden, my love and I first did meet.
I took her in my arms, and to her, I gave kisses sweet,"

Boyd and the Doctor crossed the room and eased the door open. In the backroom Daisy sat up with a guitar in her hands and her friend, Juana Bell Irvin, sat on the edge of the bed listening. Daisy continued to sing:

"She bade me take life easy just as the leaves fall from the tree.
But I being young and foolish, with my darling did not agree."

It was then that Daisy followed Juana Bell's eyes and stopped playing as she saw the two men at the door.

"You are doing much better, I see," Dr. Askew said.

"Yes, Doctor," Daisy smiled as she set the guitar down on her lap. "Juana Bell brought me my guitar."

"Where did you learn to play?" Boyd asked.

"My Uncle Wilhelm. I went to live with him after my parents died of the fever."

"He was a music teacher," Juana Bell offered.

"Played the piano, violin, harp, guitar, and I always thought, anything," Daisy said with pride.

"And sing?" Boyd asked.

"Oh, my, yes. He had a beautiful voice. He told me anyone could sing — even people who say they can't. He said it was like riding a horse. You just had to learn how."

Dr. Askew sat down in the chair beside the bed and lifted one of Daisy's sleeves. He examined the scabs and healing stitches on her arm. "I took more stitches than may have been necessary," he explained, "— hoping to minimize the scarring."

"I feel them stretch when I play," she said.

"A couple of more days and we can start taking them out."

"That sounds like fun," Daisy smiled.

"It won't hurt," the Doctor assured her.

"That would be nice for a change."

"What was that song?" Boyd asked.

"Down By The Sally Garden. It's an old Irish song. Uncle Wilhelm knew a thousand of them."

"And he taught them to you?"

Daisy chuckled and winked at Juana Bell. "That and a whole lot more."

Boyd got the meaning. He said, "Your uncle. Wasn't he in the war?"

"He had a club foot, and they wouldn't take him. At least he had a home and a place for me to go."

"But he — he took advantage of you?"

"Well," Daisy shrugged, "I started it. He was a 40-year-old bachelor, and I was 16, very curious — and horny. I didn't understand it back then, but that's who I was. He taught me — no, I think we learned everything together. He did teach me how to sing and play — and the important things. You might say he played me like a violin."

"He took advantage of you?" Boyd asked.

"I'd never say that. If what we did was wrong — a sin — I'm as much to blame as he was."

"Where is he now?"

"Dead. They finally decided they needed him in the Army. He was killed in his first battle. He left me his house — which I had to sell — and then when the money became no good — well, there was only one way I knew how to make a living."

Juana Bell nodded her understanding.

"This is his guitar, and his collection of songs — they're all I have left of him."

* * *

When the trial resumed, the District Attorney decided he had no other questions for Sheriff Danforth.

Less Burber called freedman Percy Early to the stand. The man was administered the oath and sat in the witness chair.

"Mr. Early," Burber began, "are you an acquaintance of Vander Osby?"

"I ain't sayin'."

"Your honor, everyone in town has seen Mr. Early with Mr. Osby. But can you instruct the witness to answer the question?"

"Objection," Hamlin Cranford said. "The witness has a right to assert his 5th Amendment right not to incriminate himself."

"Agreed," Less said. "But the witness has not invoked his privilege."

"He needs an attorney," Cranford said. "Your Honor, could you explain to the witness his rights."

"Mr. Early," said Judge Waberton as he leaned toward the witness. "Under our constitution, you have the right not to say anything that might prove or even involve you in any criminal activity. All you have to do is say, 'I refuse to answer claiming my rights under the 5th Amendment."

"I do that," Early said. "Fifth adend..."

"Amendment," the Judge said.

"To any question you have," Early said to Less Burber.

It took only an instant to say, "Then, Mr. Early, you do not know who shot Mr. Vander Osby because you were not there?"

Early was caught. He looked at Osby, who wasn't sure what to signal to his number 2.

Eventually, Early said, "The Sheriff shot him."

"How do you know that?"

"The 5th — thing."

"You won't tell us if you were there, but you want us to believe you know who shot Mr. Osby?"

When Early didn't answer, Less Burber said, "No more questions, Your Honor."

"The prosecution has no questions for this witness," District Attorney Cranford said.

Early, feeling untouchable, walked over to the bailiff and reclaimed his pistol and his knife. He returned to the back of the courtroom and assumed his defiant stance.

"Defense," the Judge asked. "Your next witness?"

"The defense calls Dr. Emmet Askew."

The physician stepped forward, took the oath, and the witness chair.

"Doctor, you were called to the county jail on the night in question, were you not?"

"I was."

"Please explain to the jury what you saw there that night."

"I was summoned by Deputy Boyd to treat the wound of a freedman being held in protective custody."

"Did you know the patient?"

"No, I never got his name."

"Was he locked in a cell?"

"No. He and three others, including the last witness, Mr. Early, were in the cell together, but the door was not locked. The one I treated had been wounded in the right forearm. I was able to stop the bleeding, clean the wound, and dress it."

"Was there anyone else in the jail that night?"

"The Sheriff and Deputy Boyd, of course, but also Mr. Vander Osby in another cell."

"Did you speak to Mr. Osby?"

"No, sir. I had no reason to interact with him."

"After you treated the patient, what happened?"

"Nothing. I left the jail after the Sheriff told me to submit a bill to the county. I had another patient at my office."

CHAPTER 17

"The defense calls Mr. Hartsel Zaddach."

A self-confident, pare shaped man of 55 with a droopy mustache, white hair, and long fingers stepped forward carrying a square case slightly larger than a doctor's bag. The man stated his full name for the court record and was sworn in.

"Mr. Zaddach," Less Burber asked, "what is your profession and your background?"

The man's voice easily filled the courtroom with a booming, clear sound.

"I am a gunsmith. My office is over on Dallas street, and I've been there since the war. I've been working at this for almost 30 years. I was an armorer, but worked at my craft, too."

"And what does your craft include?"

"I design, make, maintain, and repair all types of firearms from little single-shot pistols to large bore rifles and shotguns. In the last few years, I've been modifying cap and ball guns to use cartridges. I also make and sell ammunition for most of the weapons available these days."

Less went to the evidence table and picked up the deformed bullet submitted as Prosecution Exhibit A, the slug Dr. Givens had taken from Lander Osby's leg. The defense attorney handed the piece of lead to the witness.

"Mr. Zaddach, what can you tell us about this item?"

Looking it over the item, the gunsmith announced, "It's a bullet. I'd say a .36 caliber. But it's been mangled."

"Are you sure?"

"I can tell by what shape is left of it that it was a bullet. Let me get my scale, and I'll tell you more."

From inside his case, Hartsel Zaddach pulled out a balance scale. He placed it on the ledge beside his chair, turning it so the jury could see both tiny chains suspended trays of the device. He put the lead Less Burber had given him and put it on one tray. From his bag, he produced a wooden box. Removing the box revealed a series of small weights arranged in predrilled holes, one for each size. He selected one and placed it on the empty side of the scale. The two units balanced, moving the arrow at the top of the bar connecting the trays to the center mark at the top of the scale.

"This is a .36 caliber ball or slug. All of it. Nothing is missing. It's an exact match to my official 80-grain weight. I'd say it was a round ball between 0.375 and 0.380 inches."

"Is this a popular caliber?"

"It is."

"Can you name some of the weapons which use it?"

"The '38 to1841 Paterson Colt Number 5 — the Colt '51 and '61 Navy revolvers, the '62 Police Models and Pocket Pistol Models, the Remington '54 and '58, the LeMat 9 shot revolver — uh, the Colt's '37 Ring Lever revolving rifle — and as many derringers as you can count on both hands."

"Are there many of those in Jefferson?" Less standing by the jury box.

"I think I can name every man or woman in town who has one or who has bought ammunition for one or had one repaired in the past five years. I sell more .36 caliber loads than any other. Even cartridges now that the folks are switching over to them."

"Is there any way to determine which type of gun might have fired this slug?"

"Not that I know of."

Less walked over to his table and picked up two boxes of ammunition.

"This, Your Honor, is a box of .36 caliber ball and box of .36 caliber cartridge ammunition I purchased at Tidyman's Mercentail this morning. I would like to have the witness extract the bullet from the cartridge and weight it and then have him weigh a .36 ball."

"Your Honor," District Attorney Hamlin Cranford said, standing up. "For the sake of time, the State will stipulate that the bullet that Mr. Osby was shot with was a .36 caliber. Can we please proceed?"

"Yes, Mr. Burber," Judge Waberton said to the defense attorney with a pained expression. "You have made your point. Do you have anything else?"

"Yes, I do, Your Honor." Less returned the boxes to his table and picked up 2 boards that were lying beneath. "Mr. Zaddach, do you recognize these boards?"

"Those are the two floorboards you ask me to remove from the first cell in Sheriff Danforth's jail."

"And what did I tell you when you removed them?"

"Only that they were in the cell where Zander Osby was shot."

"Correct. Now, please look at these boards. Tell me what you see?"

The gunsmith checked each of the boards and then stood them up beside his chair.

"I can see both boards are several years old — and that each is sunbleached on end. This second one only halfway across but sunbleached just the same?"

"Do you have any ideas why that would be?"

"Well, when I was pulling these boards up, I noticed that the light from the cell window fell across both of them."

"What time of day was this?"

"It was close to sunset. I didn't check my watch, but I'd say around 6:30 or so — give or take a few minutes."

"And why is this second board only bleached sun part of the way?"

"That's where the window stopped letting the light in."

"Can you tell the jury anything about the cell window?"

"It looked to me like someone had shot through that window with a shotgun. There were pellet holes in walls and marks on the bars.

"Anything else you can tell us about these two boards?"

"They both have bullets in them." Zaddach pointed out the holes in both boards.

"Can you pull one of them out?"

The gunsmith pulled a knife and a pair of plyers from his toolbox and did so as Less Burber asked, "Is there anything else you can tell us about these bullets?"

"From the holes, I'd say they were shot from a high angle."

"For example?"

"Off a ladder — or a horse maybe — outside the window into the cell."

Zaddach had the first slug free. He moved to weigh it on the scale while Less took the other board to the Judge to examine. He also showed it to the District Attorney and then passed it down each row for every jury member to see.

On the scale, the removed slug balanced on the scale exactly where the one Dr. Givens had removed from Vander Osby's leg.

While the jury looked over the board, its sun-bleached surface, and the bullet hole's angle, Less went to the evidence table and picked up Sheriff Danforth's pistol. He removed one cartridge and handed it to the gunsmith. Zaddach pulled the lead from the cartridge and put it on his scale. The scale dipped to the weight of the bullet.

"What does this tell you, Mr. Zaddach?"

Zaddach picked up the distorted slug from Osby's leg and the bullet from the Sheriff's gun.

"That this slug did not come from that gun."

CHAPTER 18

The jury was back within a half-hour. The verdict was unanimous, "Not guilty."

Judge Waberton found the man in the nice suit and frowned before he announced, "Court adjourned." He banged his gavel.

Boyd didn't even shake hands with Sheriff Danforth but headed for the door where he intercepted Price Early before the freedman could get out. With his pistol in his hand and the hammer cocked, Boyd said, "Price Early, you are under arrest for murder."

"Who'd I kill?"

"Doctor Julius Givens. The boy you sent to get Doctor Askew with the false story about Mrs. Grover needing the Doctor because her baby was coming — he identified you as the one who gave him two silver dollars to deliver the message."

Keeping his pistol trained on Early, Boyd relieved the man of his pistol and snatched the knife from his boot.

Across the courtroom, Sheriff Danforth had shaken hands with Less Burber before stepping over to the evidence table and reclaiming his gunbelt and pistol. With his pistol cocked he stepped up to Vander Osby, saying, "You're under arrest."

"For what?" Vander almost spat the words out.

"The attempted murder of Daisy Marie Philpot — with a horsewhip."

The courtroom was frozen in place listening.

"Your Honor," Vander said after seeing what was happening with Price Early, "you can't have us put back in that jail. I don't care what the jury said. He tried to kill me — he'll do it again."

"How about the city jail, Your Honor?" Hamlin Cranford asked. "Marshal Roggy could take charge of these two men — who we must remember are innocent until proven guilty."

"If they were in Roggy's jail, they'd be gone by tonight," Sheriff Danforth said.

"I have a compromise," Col. L. Lavern Pardee called out. Standing as tall as the short man could, the commanding officer of Fort Jefferson said, "I could secure them in the fort's stockade. Is the word of the United States Army sufficient for you, Sheriff Danforth?"

Corwin Danforth looked over at Boyd, who was holding Price Early at the front door. Boyd didn't have a word to say.

"I'll take them to jail," the Sheriff finally said. "And I'll await a squad of your troops to escort them to your stockade."

"I can agree to that," Col. Pardee said.

"I'll go along and ensure everything is done correctly," Cranford said.

"And I expect a proper prosecution," Sheriff Danforth said evenly to the District Attorney.

"Are you questioning my ethics or my abilities?" the District Attorney angrily asked.

"I think the trial we just went through speaks to both," Danforth said.

* * *

Boyd and Sheriff Danforth got Vander Osby and Price Early to jail only moments before a carpetbagger lawyer, Pierre Harr, walked into the office. Harr was a sloped shouldered, flabby man with a high forehead and stringy charcoal gray hair.

"I would like to see my clients," Harr said as Boyd and Corwin closed the door to the cells.

The two lawmen exchanged looks and a laugh.

"That didn't take long," Sheriff Danforth said with a smile.

"Here I thought bad news traveled fast," Boyd said. "Sleaze seems to lead the pack."

Boyd opened the door and allowed the attorney into Vander's cell.

Hanging up the keys back in the office, Boyd said, "After all you've been through, don't you need a bath — supper and a good night's sleep?"

"As a matter of fact, I think I would," the Sheriff said, taking his hat off a peg by the door.

"I'll see these two and their shyster get to the fort."

"I'll see you back here in the morning, Deputy."

"Good night, Sheriff."

Half an hour later a detail of four armed soldiers arrived with a shave-tail lieutenant in charge.

"Sir, these men are now my responsibility," the young man said, snapping Boyd a smart salute.

"Well, I'll just walk along with you to make sure nothing goes wrong."

The detail marched with the two prisoners and their lawyer to Fort Jefferson.

The fort looked like an early colonist's log fort minus the parapets. Local pine trees made up the facility's walls. The double doors were open, and Colonel L. Lavern Pardee met the detail at the entrance. The Lieutenant halted the detail inside the fort's threshold and exchanged salutes with his commanding officer.

"See, the prisoners are escorted to the stockade," Colonel Pardee told the young officer.

"Yes, sir."

Boyd stood outside as the post doors were closed. There was nothing else for him to do.

* * *

Following his supper, Boyd went to The Bale of Cotton to inspect the progress of the changes he called for. He was surprised at the newly painted walls and the nearly completed stage.

"I didn't think I'd like it," partner Layman Haverstick said, walking up beside Boyd, "but I do. Does class the place up."

Boyd was pleased himself. "It's turning out better than I expected."

"Two of our bartenders, Matthew and Thomas, used to work in minstrel shows before the war. They knew exactly what was needed. The curtains are being made and should be up the day after tomorrow. All we're going to need is a couple of coats of shellac on the stage and an extra day or two for it to dry."

"Thank you, Layman," Boyd said, offering his hand to his partner.

Shaking hands, Layman said, "I'm so impressed with it that I decided to pay for part of it myself — you're still getting the biggest bill — but I'll pick up 40 percent or so."

"Thank you, partner."

A hush came over the room. Boyd turned to see Vander Osby and Price Early standing near the door, looking over the changes.

"Nice," Vander said. "I still think you're goin' t' loose money without my girls ..."

Boyd cut him off. "What are you two doing out of the stockade?"

"It's all perfectly legal, Deputy. With Mr. Harr's help, we've been arraigned by Judge Waberton, and both Price and myself are out on bail. The Judge's calendar was full so the trial won't be for two months." Osby took a pull on his fresh cigar.

"Swift justice my ass," Boyd said. "Neither one of you are welcome here — ever. Get out, or I'll throw you out!"

"Don't get excited. We're going."

"I ain't scared of him," Early said, stepping away from Osby and getting ready to draw."

"Now, now," Osby said. "We are on our best behavior. It's part of our release agreement. We only stopped by to see you, Boyd, so you wouldn't be surprised when you see us around."

"Stay away from Daisy," Boyd said in a low growl.

"Of course. Should anything happen to her, I'm sure I would be blamed for it. And I've never laid a hand on her — professionally — or otherwise." Then with a nasty grin, Osby said, "In court it's going to be her word against mine. The word of a whore against an established businessman. Who do you think a jury will believe?"

Osby turned and walked out, using his cane, and Price Early backed out, still ready for a gunfight.

CHAPTER 19

Boyd was in the Sheriff's Office when a refreshed Corwin Danforth came in smiling the next morning.

"You've not heard about Osby and Price being out on bail, I gather," Boyd said, pouring a coffee from the pot on the potbelly stove.

"Oh, yes," the Sheriff said as he hung up his hat. "I even expected as much."

"And the trial not being held for two months?"

"Judge Waberton at his finest. Did Vander get Pierre Harr for a lawyer?"

"How'd you know that?"

"Birds of a feather." The Sheriff took the offered coffee from Boyd.

"This being the first of the month, Boyd, we need to collect county taxes."

"Taxes?"

"It's not so bad. You get to meet the local merchants and give them a campaign poster."

"I don't have any campaign posters," Boyd said.

"Thought not. So I took the liberty of having some made up for you." Sheriff Danforth pulled the tax ledger out of the desk and

THE HUSSY AND THE HARDCASE

handed it to Boyd. "We'll stop by the Jimp and pick some posters up. I'll let you pay for them. Then it's time for us to go door to door."

* * *

Ward Taylor was the editor and publisher of the Jimplecute. The bowlegged pockmarked faced publisher was 40, and wore a wide smile. The man's intelligence was shown through his flecked eyes that took in everything. He and Boyd knew each other because of the Deputy's hands-off investment in the paper a few years before.

The man wore a green eyeshade and opened his cash box as the Sheriff wrote a receipt for the taxes.

"Is the kid who identified Price Early safe?" the editor asked, paying the Sheriff and getting the posters on top of his cluttered desk.

"He is," the Sheriff said. "And we're not saying where."

"And I'm not asking," Taylor answered, setting the stack of posters on the stand-up reception table.

The boy was being looked after by the Titus County Sheriff in Mt. Pleasant, 80 miles northwest of Jefferson.

The election posters had a professionally drawn sketch of Boyd under the bold lettered word, "ELECT," and the equally cast words "FOR SHERIFF" beneath. The rest of the page read, "A bold man for honest justice!"

"Good work," Sheriff Danforth said, studying one of the sheets. "Pay the man, Deputy."

"No charge," Ward Taylor said. "Consider it a campaign contribution." He handed Boyd the stack of string-bound posters.

"Much obliged," was all Boyd could manage before he headed for the door. Sheriff Danforth winked and nodded with a grin behind Boyd's back to the publisher. Ward waved off the gesture and went back to work.

* * *

From the other 2 newspapers to meat markets, general stores, barbers, undertaker, a dozen saloons, 2 banks, they went. The called on 4 liveries, 3 blacksmiths, 2 dressmakers, a freight office and riverboat shipper, 3 hotels, 5 doctors, 3 dentists, 6 eateries and restaurants, boarding houses, hotels, and a photographer. The Sheriff collected the taxes and Boyd entered the amount in the ledger and left a poster. From Austin street over to Dallas, they went. Then North on Polk and back down Vale, and up Market.

One building, a 3 story brick structure on Common, looked like a bank or hotel as they approached. An ornamental set of double doors with etched glass and a polished knob greeted them at the top of four steps. It was The Alcove. Boyd flipped through the ledger he carried searching for the name when Sheriff Danforth reached over and closed the book.

"This is listed as 'Miscellaneous,'" he said as the door opened, and a towering black man in a suit and tie opened the door. "Back of the book."

"Sheriff Danforth," the man said inside, stepping aside for the two lawmen to enter. "We was 'pectin' you."

"Malachi, this is my deputy, Boyd Spanner."

"Deputy Spanner, welcome to The Alcove," Malachi said, dipping his head.

Boyd nodded his greeting in exchange.

"Miss Vel is in her office. If you gentlemen will follow me."

Malachi led the way down the shiny hardwood floors, past an expansive parlor with plush and expensive furnishings.

Althea Velvet was known around Jefferson. Somewhere in her mid-30s, she dressed in a high collar, long-sleeved lace dress. She had creamy skin, obsidian eyes, and sable hair that was piled and coffered perfectly on the top of her head. She had a distinct widow's peak which gave her the look of a living cameo.

Boyd knew who Althea was and removed his hat following the Sheriff's example as they entered a lovely appointed office. She smiled and handed Danforth an envelope.

"Punctual as usual, Sheriff."

"Miss Velvet," he said, adding, "do you know Deputy Boyd Spanner?"

"Not personally," she said, "but I've seen him around town and know the miscarriage of justice heaped upon him. Deputy," she nodded.

"Ma'am," Boyd said.

"Will you offer me a couple of those posters?" she asked, gesturing to Boyd's bundle.

"Of course," he said and gave her 3.

"Oh, I think I can handle more than that," she said. She reached out and pulled out a quarter of his remaining pack. "I'll see that these go where they can do the most good," she said with a wink.

"Thank you," Boyd said awkwardly.

"Think nothing of it. We here know about what all you've done for Daisy — from Godfrey Mull to her current condition. You are a unique man, Mr. Spanner. It would be our honor to have you become our next sheriff. You will have big boots to fill," she said, glancing at Danforth and then back at Boyd, "but the faith he has in you is not, I believe, misplaced."

"Kind of you to say so, ma'am."

"Please. Make it Althea. I've tried to get the good Sheriff to call me that for a few years, but he seems to prefer to keep things more formal."

"I would be happy to call you Althea if you'll call me Boyd."

"Said and done," she said with a small smile.

CHAPTER 20

The last stop of the day was Vander Osby's bordello, The Dove's Roost. It was a block away but the clapboard two-story building spoke to the different world the services offered here compared to those at The Alcove. Sheriff Danforth knocked on the door, and it was answered by Price Early, Osby's right-hand man.

"What do you want?" Early asked with a sneer.

"Taxes," the Sheriff said.

Early clenched his jaw before he walked away from the open door allowing the Sheriff and Boyd to enter.

A spacious parlor to the left was furnished with couches and chairs that were neither matched nor of the same style. They looked more than a little worn. Four women in dressing gowns or corsets and stockings lounged there smoking cigarettes and, in one case, a pipe. None looked inviting, although they were excessively made up.

A woman's scream was heard down the hall following loud crying and another cry in pain. The Sheriff and Boyd started to charge down the hall when Price Early blocked their way.

"Nothin' that goes on here is any of ya' b'iness."

"If a woman is being hurt...," Boyd began but was cut off by Early.

"Some men like it rough. And the girls know they're bein' paid fer it."

"Where is Vander?" the Sheriff asked.

"He'll be here in a minute. Jest hold ya' horses."

A full minute later, Vander Osby stepped out of a room at the end of the hall, lacing his belt into his pants' loops. He continued his task as he walked up the hall toward the two lawmen.

"Is it that time again?" Osby asked.

"What was going on back there?" Boyd wanted to know.

Osby glanced over his shoulder and then turned back to Boyd.

"These bitches have to be kept in line. It takes the strap every now and again. But they seem to get the message."

Vander reached into the inside pocket of his plaid coat and pulled out his wallet. He counted out the amount of his county taxes and handed it to the Sheriff but didn't let go of it even when Danforth had taken hold of it.

"You know," Osby said with an evil grin, "some people would consider this a bribe."

"Some people would consider this a whorehouse, too," the Sheriff said.

Osby dropped his smile and let go of the greenbacks.

"Does Althea Velvet pay the same thing I do?"

"To the penny," Danforth said.

"Stupid bitch. She paid for the Presbyterian's to get a new roof after that storm last year tore their old one off. And do you think they'd ever let her darken their door?"

Boyd opened his tax ledger as the Sheriff pulled a poster from Boyd's stack and handed it to Osby. Osby read it, wadded it up, and threw it on the floor. Gesturing with his head, Osby motioned for Early to follow him. The two left through the front door.

After Boyd had made his notation, he saw that the Sheriff was headed down the hall towards the room from which Osby had come. Boyd followed him. No one attempted to stop them.

Danforth tapped on the door before he opened it and stopped. Boyd stepped up behind the Sheriff.

Inside the room was a naked woman with whelps all over her body.

She was clutching her robe to her as she cried. Through tears, she said, "No more."

"It's all right," Danforth said.

Boyd pushed past the Sheriff to the bed where the woman was curled into a fetal position.

"Juana Bell, why did he do this?" Boyd asked.

Through her tears and her fears, she recognized Boyd and let down her guard, still awash in tears. It took her a moment to be able to speak. When she could, it was only slightly above a whisper when she said, "Cause I helped Daisy."

"If you sign a complaint, I'll arrest the som'bitch for assault," the Sheriff said.

"No! No!" Juana Bell said, sitting up. "I got no place t' go." She dropped her robe to display her nakedness. "I'm jest a whore. He can do anything he wants to me."

"No, he can't," Boyd said. "Get dressed. You're coming with us, Juana Bell. Nobody's ever going to do this to you again."

"I can't!" she wailed.

"Yes, you can. Get dressed. I'm taking you to Doc Askew's."

Juana Bell stopped crying as she considered Boyd's words. She swallowed, wiped her eyes, and gently pulled on her robe over her body's marks. She opened a wardrobe and took out a dress to put on over the gown. She then collected the few other items in the wardrobe, put them in a bag, and stepped into her only shoes. She followed Danforth out to the hall. Boyd was right behind.

Not one of the parlor's astonished women said a word as the three passed out the front door.

* * *

After a week of healing, Juana Bell was up and around with Daisy. Dr. Askew talked to Juana Bell about becoming his helper. He used the words "nurse" and "mid-wife."

Daisy was almost back to normal. She kept singing to her friend, and one day Boyd brought two of the bartenders from The Bale to meet her. One brought his banjo and the other a stand-up string bass.

* * *

On the following Friday before the election, Jefferson was blanked with Vander Osby For Sheriff Posters pasted to every available wall and post. At noon, a parade featuring a circus company, elephant and all, started out coming down Pope and turning on to Austin. The blaring brass band led the way, circus performers did cartwheels, and caged wild animals were displayed on wagons. All the while, Vander Osby posters were handed out and scattered into the air by any parade member with free hands.

A barker used a megaphone announced the opening of the circus West of town beginning that night. All were invited — free. The crowd followed the parade and watched the erection of a massive tent.

That same night after the end of the circuit, Layman Haverstick lowered the room lights and turned up those on the stage. A small crowd hushed, Layman stepped out from behind the curtains and spoke.

"Tonight I want to introduce to you — The Jefferson Riverport Trio. I think you're going to like this, gentlemen.

The banjo player stepped out and said, "Good evening. My name is Matthew — not to be confused with the apostle." Next, the bass player emerged. He announced, "Hi. I'm Thomas — but certainly not the saint." There were some laughs at this point.

Then Daisy stepped out, holding her guitar. She wore a high neck, long-sleeved dress with some rhinestone-lined diamond-shaped holes across her chest and down her arms. She stepped in between the men and said, "Most of you know me as Daisy — but my real name is Mary. And I'm certainly not a —," she stopped as the room burst into laughter.

CHAPTER 21

The Jefferson Riverport Trio began strumming an upbeat tune.
"*One,*" the banjo player Matthew sang.
"*Two,*" added quickly, Daisy.
"*And three,*" sang Thomas, the bass player.
Together the group sang,
"*...jolly coachmen sat in an English tavern.*
Three jolly coachmen sat in an English Tavern.
Matthew sang, "*And they decided...*"
Daisy joined him, singing, "*And they decided...*"
Thomas added his harmony, and all three sang, "*And they decided —*
to have another flagon."
Using the same pattern, they sang the verses:
"*Here's to the girl who steals a kiss*
And runs to tell her mother.
Here's to the girl who steals a kiss
And runs to tell her mother.
She's a foolish, foolish thing,
She's a foolish, foolish thing,
She's a foolish, foolish thing —
For she'll not get another."

. . .

"Here's to the girl who steals a kiss
And stays to steal another.
Here's to the girl who steals a kiss
And stays to steal another.
She's a boon to all mankind,
She's a boon to all mankind,
She's a boon to all mankind —
For she'll soon be a mother!"

The crowd loved it. They clapped, laughed, and roared their approval. The noise drew others near The Bale, and the crowd grew.

The trio sang Skewball The Race Horse, Banks Of The Ohio, Sweet Betsy from Pike, Scarborough Fair, Danny Boy, Silver Dagger, and Golden Slippers. As an encore, they sang The Yellow Rose Of Texas.

The performance was a great success, and even compared to the free circus, it was the most memorable event of the day. And there was nothing said in The Bale that night about the campaign for Sheriff. The focus was only on the three singers.

Nothing needed to be said. The men understood what Boyd had done because Layman had told everyone about the changes he wanted.

* * *

At Doc Askew's office after the show, Daisy was beaming. She was telling Juana Bell all about it.

"I knew you were going to be great. Remember I heard you practicing," said Juana Bell, who was recovered now but still staying in the doctor's office with Daisy.

There was a tap at the door, and Boyd stuck his head in.

"Congratulations," he said and stepped in, looking around. "Where's the doctor?"

"Out on a call," Juana Bell said.

"He just left you alone?"

Juana Bell revealed a small five-shot revolver, a Remington Rimfire

5 shot .38 from a pocket in the folds of her dress. "Not exactly alone," she grinned.

Boyd walked back to the front door and locked it before returning to the two women. He told them, "I plan to bunk on the couch out in the front office until Osby's trial is over."

"I have my gun, too," Daisy said, producing the Derringer she had threatened Boyd with when he first returned to town.

"I know, but I still don't trust Osby — or Price Early. They might figure Juana Bell has decided to testify against Vander."

"I have," Juana Bell said.

"Are you sure?" Boyd asked.

"Oh, I'm scared — but I want to do this for Daisy."

"You've done way more than I ever needed," Daisy said. "If you hadn't called Dr. Askew the night Osby tried to kill me, I'd be dead now."

"And instead, you're a singer, now" Juana Bell beamed. "I am so proud of you. How much are you gettting paid?"

"Twelve hundred dollars a week — split three ways. How's that?" Boyd asked.

"I used to make that much on a good night," Daisy said. "But I'm never going back to that. It will do me just fine."

"If you continue to bring in the crowds, I'll see you all get a raise — and quickly."

Daisy like that. She looked at Juana Bell, she said, "You shouldn't go back either Juana Bell."

"Honey, the doctor's been very nice to me — but — Osby is right. I am a whore, a hussy, a harlot — always will be."

"You don't have to be," Daisy insisted.

"I can't sing — and I can't stay here. I'll have to go somewhere else or Osby will kill me. I know that. But I've found out that not all men are bad. And I like men. A few have even asked me to marry them. Maybe the next one that does, I'll take him up on it — where ever I am."

"I wish you'd think it over. Doc Askew says you'd be a good nurse," Daisy said.

"I'd be putting his life in danger, too, if I stayed. I can't do that."

THE HUSSY AND THE HARDCASE

Juana Bell turned to Boyd and asked, "What I don't understand is why you are going out of your way for us? I never saw you at the Roost — even before you went to prison."

Boyd looked at the two women closely and then sat down on the straight back chair.

"My mother was a whore," he said slowly. "After my father was killed right at the beginning of the war, I lied about my age and joined up, too. I never thought about my mother and what she was going through. I wanted to get revenge for my father."

"Did you?" Daisy asked.

"I killed a lot of Yankees — but none of it ever seemed to be enough. Nothing made up for his being killed."

"And your mother?"

"Father sent her all of his pay, but after he died, the money stopped. I sent all of mine — but like many other soldiers, I don't think any of it ever made it home. She sold our place — which wasn't worth much by then. There wasn't anyone left to run a farm. She ran out of money and charity pretty soon."

"And the only thing she had left to sell was herself," Daisy finished the story.

"A story as old as history, I suppose," Boyd sighed.

"Doesn't make any difference even when it's you," Daisy said, looking over at Juana Bell.

"You took care of Daisy — and me because you couldn't do anything for your mother?"

Boyd thought about this for a moment before saying, "I never thought about it like that — but it seems like that's the way of it."

"I'm sorry for your mother, but — well, I'm glad," Juana Bell said, "for me. And I know Daisy is, too."

"Damn right," she said. "You saved my life in more ways than one. I think you could do the same for Juana Bell if she'd let you."

"He's saved me enough." I need to stand on my own feet now.

"Make sure, Juana Bell," Boyd said. "If you go back to that life — have you ever thought about asking Althea Velvet if you could work at The Alcove?"

"No, they're too classy for me. I wish I was that type — but I ain't — and I know it."

"Where will you go?" Boyd asked.

"I ain't figured that out yet. But, I'm thinkin' on it."

"Stay here a while and work for Doc," Daisy said. "You might find out you like it more than you think."

CHAPTER 22

The circus remained outside of town with free shows to dwindling crowds each night through Sunday. The traveling show was struck and packed up on Monday. But Vander Osby had paid the troop to remain in town until they had voted on Tuesday.

Election Day was the busiest day Jefferson had seen in years. Not only were the circus people still around, but new faces, both black and white, appeared. The four local churches were the election sites in town, and churches across the county were open for the same function. In Jefferson, it quickly became apparent that many of those wanting to vote did not belong in Marion County. While Marshal Roggy and his deputies showed themselves at each polling place throughout the day, the election officials decided to require proof of county residency before allowing strangers to cast a ballot. At the end of the day, these same officials compared voter logs from the different churches and discovered the names of many who had voted more than once. These names were stricken from the rolls, and an equal number of votes were withdrawn from the count. Still, by 9 PM, it was clear that Boyd Spanner had won the post of County Sheriff by a sizeable margin.

Boyd was watching The Jefferson Riverport Trio perform a new addition to their program, Shenandoah. The group had added a new song or two almost every day. Their story songs were the favorites.

Hank Newbold, a man in a suit and bowler hat, had a wad of official papers in his hand when he stepped up between Boyd and Sheriff Danforth at the bar. He was the counties, chief election official.

"Deputy," he announced as the crowd cheered at the end of the song, "it is now official. Votes are in from Kellytown, and Gray. You're our new Sheriff. Congratulations."

Boyd shook hands with Newbold, who turned toward the stage and listened a moment to the next song. "They are as good as I've heard." Newbold left through the front door.

Danforth took off his badge and said, "Let's trade badges. I'll be your deputy for about another month. Then you'll have to get someone else. I'm going fishing. Might even snag ol' Big Bill."

Boyd removed his badge and pinned on his new symbol of office. Danforth did the same.

"What will you do if you catch that alligator?" Boyd asked.

"First I'll shoot the som'bitch and then get me some boots made out of his hide."

The new Sheriff and the new Deputy shared a laugh and they both turned back to the singers on stage.

The Jefferson Riverport Trio was singing another song, new to the show, Cory, Cory. It started with a banjo lead. Then the trio sang in three-part harmony.

"There's a pine log shack in the mountains. That's where my Cory dwells.
She makes the finest mash liquor. What she doesn't drink she sells.

Well, the first time I seen darlin' Cory, she was weavin' through the woods
With a kerosene lantern on her shoulder and a satchel full of goods."

Both of the men sang,

. . .

"Please do drop-down next Monday. Please bring me a jug or five.
When the sun comes up on Tuesday, don't figure to be alive."

Daisy picked the next verse by herself.

"Don't care if you are livin'. Don't care if you are dead.
If you're gonna drink my product, then I'm gonna take your bread."

There was a banjo break, and then the trio finished up the song together.

"The last time I seen darlin' Cory, she was wandrin' thru the weeds
With a government man behind her. Gonna grab her for her deeds.

Wake up, wake up, darlin' Cory. What makes you sleep so sound?
The revenue officer's a-comin', gonna tear your still house down."

As always, the crowd loved the song stood as they applauded.

Layman shouted out before the next song could begin. "Hear ye, hear ye! We have a new Sheriff! Drinks are on the house!"

The crowd yelled their approval and rushed the bar.

It was 20 minutes before the singers could get back on track with their show. When they finished and did their encore of both The Yellow Rose of Texas and Dixie, the saloon was in a delightful roar.

Then a shot rang out, and all eyes went to Percy Early, who stood in the doorway a revolver in his hand. His bowler hat was tipped back on his head, and his flashy stickpins looked dull in the lights as they came up.

"I come for you — Sheriff Boyd Spanner!" Early slurred. "You ready to face me?"

Boyd had turned and narrowed his eyes.

"You going to start with your gun out. Afraid of a fair fight!"

"I ain't never been afraid!"

"Then put your pistol up, and let's go out in the street. There's no need of anyone here being shot when you miss."

Early laughed as he holstered his pistol — taking two tries to sleeve his weapon. "I'm faster than you — Sheriff. I seen you draw on those boys in here a while back. I'm going to kill you." Early turned and staggered outside.

Boyd slipped the thong off the hammer of his Army Remington. He followed Early into the lamp lite street.

"You ready t' die, Sheriff?" Early challenged when Boyd was 20 feet away from him.

"I've been practicing," Boyd said. "I may have been slow — but I'm faster now."

"Not fast enough."

"You'd better be quick," Boyd said, bracing himself. "I intend to gut shoot you. You're going to die hard."

"Let's jest see." Early drew.

Boyd felt the bullet whiz past his ear as he fired his first shot and then fanned two more rounds into Early's stomach. Early was thrown back and lay bleeding into the brick street. His pistol flew out of his hand, and he clutched the gushing wounds in his belly.

Holstering his pistol, Boyd walked over and stood looking down on Osby's hired killer. The crowd from The Bale and other nearby saloons circled the two men.

Early began breathing hard, and there was blood coming out of his mouth.

"Someone want to go get a doctor," Boyd said to no one in particular. "No rush. There's nothing anybody can do for him."

Early screamed in pain.

"That's the acid from your stomach burning its way through your gut," Boyd said.

"Somebody help me!" Early pleaded.

"You're already dead," Boyd told him. "You have nothing left but pain — and a place waiting for you in hell."

Early yelled and thrashed. "Somebody shoot me," he begged.

"Wouldn't be fair," Boyd said. "You're unarmed."

The gunman turned to his side and tried to reach out for his pistol, but it was too far for him to grasp. And then Boyd put a boot on it.

Price Early screamed twice more and went limp as he whizzed his last breath.

CHAPTER 23

Town Marshal Raymond Roggy burst into the Sheriff's office early the next morning clutching a newspaper.

"You killed Price Early in a gunfight on the street?"

"Haven't you read all about it?" the new Deputy asked as Sheriff Spanner looked up at the fuming Marshal.

"I had to find out about it in the Jimp! Damn it! This is my town!"

"Maybe you should spend more time on the streets of your town and off your fat ass," Danforth said.

"You want to arrest me?" Boyd asked.

All Roggy could do was shake his fist with the newspaper in it. The story, detailed with witness statements, made it clear Early was drunk and had drawn first. It was a clear case of self-defense. The veins in his thick neck bulged as his face began to look like an overripe beet. Then he spun around and stormed out with the same fury with which he had entered.

Boyd stood saying, "I think I'll take a ride up to Mt. Pleasant. There's no reason the Curee boy needs to hide out anymore."

"Good idea. Wouldn't hurt to stop in Kellytown and show the badge. Maybe say a few' Thank yous.'"

"You're still acting like I did this for me?"

"Doesn't matter, now. You're their Sheriff, too."

* * *

By the time Boyd had returned to Jefferson, it was late afternoon. He saw Deputy Danforth loading a Winchester into his saddle boot and putting a box of .44-70s in his saddlebags.

"What's up?"

"Glad you're back. Deputy Falby rode in to say Vander Osby's been seen headed along Caddo Lake. Said it looked like was carrying a heavy carpetbag. He's making a run for it is my guess. Without Price Early, I'll bet he's scared."

"Where's Falby now?"

"He'll meet us at Three Forks Bayou. That's where he's been known to do business in the past. Are you ready, or do you need to change horses?"

"No, we're good. Lead the way.

* * *

Wheaton Falby was past 60 and still wore the trousers he'd worn in the war. The former Sergeant Major sat on his yellow dun with his double-barrel .12 gauge across his saddle.

Danforth introduced him to Boyd, and the men shook hands.

"Pleased to meet you, Sgt. Major."

"Congratulations, Sheriff."

"What do we have?" Danforth asked.

"Osby's riding a big horse, and it is carrying a heavy load. But the hoof marks kinda' peter out about here. I'm sure he took one of the forks. Likely has a rowboat or a shallow canoe waiting for him down one of these three forks."

"Let's each take one," Boyd said. "Fire a shot if you need help. I'll take the middle fork."

The deputies nodded their agreement, and the three split up.

The ground was mossy and thick with weeds, but not a sign was evident of anyone having passed. At the head of the center fork Boyd thought, he saw what could have been mud slung by a horse. He rode forward about a quarter of a mile and dismounted. He left his appaloosa ground hitched and went forward on foot with his pistol drawn.

The trees were thick with Spanish moss and the water black in the approaching evening light.

Stepping around one old cypress, Boyd saw Osby tying his reins to a fallen tree branch. He stepped over to the water's edge and pulled brush aside, revealing a shallow draft Caddo canoe. He managed to heave the craft into the dark water with its bow on land. He returned to his horse and untied the carpetbag from the pommel of his saddle.

Boyd had silently worked his way to within about 20 feet or so before the horse snorted. The new Sheriff pulled his pistol and cocked it.

Osby finished untying the bag but didn't turn around until Boyd said, "Going somewhere, Vander? You forget you have a court date?"

The heavyset men let the bag down until he was holding it in his left hand as he turned. As he extended his right arm toward Boyd, an over and under, two barreled .44 Derringer sprang from his sleeve to his hand.

"I can kill you as easily as you can kill me," Osby said. "Two .44 slugs will do a lot of damage. So you hold it right there."

"I can't let you go," Boyd said.

"You can't stop me unless you're willing to die to do it."

Osby toted his bag to the canoe and muscled it into the bow. He then used his left hand to ease the canoe into the water.

At that distance, Boyd knew Vander couldn't miss. But neither could he.

Osby stepped into the canoe and used his left hand to maneuver the paddle and move the craft away from the bank.

A few more feet and Boyd knew the Derringer's accuracy wasn't going to be very good. Boyd planned to let the whoremaster back up a few more feet and then fire.

But before Osby got that far away, there was a small ripple and then a surge from the water beside the boat. A monster alligator, it had to be the one they called Big Bill, propelled himself out of the dark water with his jagged jaws wide open. They clamped down on Osby and wrenched the man out of the boat into the swamp. There was thrashing and frailing as the gator twirled Osby around and around and finally under the water.

A ripple from its tail was the last sign of either the prehistoric amphibian or Vander Osby.

Boyd could have shot the monster, but he knew it had already crushed Osby's ribs. The man didn't even have time to fire the deadly weapon in his fist. After a few more moments as the water settled, Boyd holstered his revolver, unhitched Osby's horse, and walked her back to his appaloosa. When he had both animal's reins in his hand, he pulled his Remmington and fired a shot in the air.

What neither the new Sheriff nor either of his deputies could know was that for years to come, Caddo fisherman would report snagging pieces of plaid cloth on their hooks. But Vander Osby's body never turned up.

CHAPTER 24

Sheriff Boyd Spanner stood at the door of The Alcove as Malachi opened the front door. It was late morning.

"Sheriff Spanner," the big man said.

"Malachi," Boyd greeted him but didn't step in. "I'd like to see Miss Velvet. If she's entertaining, I'll come back another time."

"Miss Velvet has never entertained," Malachi said. "Not in all the years I've know'd her — and that was since she was a child. She's in her office, and I'm sure she would be proud to meet with you."

"Thank you," Boyd said, following the man to the lady's office. Malachi tapped on the door and waited for a reply to come from inside before he said, "Miss Velvet, the new Sheriff is here to see you."

"Come in."

Malachi closed the door from the outside as Boyd took the chair the lady offered.

After a moment Boyd said, "Without Vander here, what's going to happen to The Roost?"

"I understand what you're saying, Sheriff, but I am not interested in expanding my business. And not to disparage any of the women at The Roost, I have to say they are not the kind who would fit in well here."

"I was kind of afraid of that," Boyd said. "Somebody will take it over — and I'm afraid for the women who work there."

"Very considerate, Sheriff. But I'm not greedy, and I know when I have enough. To seek more would be — let's just say I'm not interested." She studied him a moment and then said, "The reason I'm in here is because I knew women who had no other choice — but none of them understood business. I did. Perhaps it was a wicked thing to do, but I was and am trying to help."

"I understand," Boyd said with a sigh. He got up but paused at the door and turned back. "Let me make one more suggestion. What if one of the women there could take over The Roost and run it?"

"That would be an excellent solution. The problem is most of these woman don't think enough of themselves after doing this a while. They can't see themselves as anything but a whore."

"Yes, I've seen that."

"But someone could — with some help — excuse the expression — become a madame."

"Nothing to excuse, Sheriff. A spade is a spade."

The two stood looking at each other, and then the lady spoke again.

"Perhaps I would offer — a new owner — some suggestions."

"That would be wonderful. Could you?"

"First of all —," she paused and called out, "Malachi! Could you please come in here?"

A moment later, there was a tap at the door, and the big black man opened the door.

"Yes, ma'am?"

"Where is your brother?"

"Zechariah? He's working for Captain Shreve tryin' t' clear the river."

"Do you think he'd like to do the same kind of work you do?"

"Zack is a kindly soul, ma'am, but he can be hell on wheels, beggin' your pardon, when he sees things that ain't right."

"Get hold of him and have him see me. We're going to see if we can't get The Roost off to a new start."

Malachi beamed. "Yes, ma'am. I'll get him here as quick's I can." The big man withdrew.

"I wouldn't put a great deal of hope into this, Sheriff. From my experience, with very few exceptions, most of the women who go from, what they call, *'working on the line'* to being the owner and *madame*, begin to think they are better than those who work for me. Sometimes it gets as bad as it was under Vander Osby."

"I think it's at least worth trying."

"You find someone you think would work out, like Miss Juana Bell Irvin ..."

"You know her?"

"I've seen her around. She's impressed me as someone with a good head on her shoulders — probably better than she knows. But she should take Dr. Askew's offer and become his nurse."

"You are well informed."

"Pillow talk, Sheriff." Then she added, "Perhaps someone – from outside would be a good choice. Leave that to me."

"Would it be too much to ask for you to have a talk with Juana Bell. I think she would listen to you in a way she never would with me."

"Yes. I would be happy to, Sheriff."

* * *

The Trio performed every other day, twice on Saturdays, with Sundays off. They drew in such business that Boyd doubled their salary.

A company of traveling actors arrived by paddle wheel, and for a week, they alternated with the Trio. A play one day, the Trio the next. The day before they were to leave, Daisy ask Boyd to meet with the Trio and the acting company's manager, a man named Fremont Pettyjohn.

Pettyjohn dressed flamboyantly, a cravat instead of a tie and a plantation straw hat. They met in the saloon's office on the second floor.

"I have a proposal for your singers, Mr. Spanner," Pettyjohn said. "They make such an impressive alternate to my actors, I thought about hiring them to travel with us. It would improve the billing and allow me to offer clients two totally different and yet attractive alternatives."

THE HUSSY AND THE HARDCASE

Boyd looked to the banjo and the base players. "Matt, Thomas, what do you think? You've both worked with traveling companies."

"If the pay is right it would be the kind of thing we've dreamed about — except," Matt said.

"Daisy, what do you think?" Thomas asked.

"I'm confident enough about what we do — but how does it work?"

"I'll take care of all the arrangements," Pettyjohn said. "I'll book the dates and arrange for accommodations."

"And where would we go?" Daisy asked.

"We're on our way to San Antonio by way of Ft. Worth. Then we're scheduled in Galveston and New Orleans. From there, we can travel by riverboat all the way to Chicago — then Philadelphia, New York, Boston, Charleston — down the whole Eastern seaboard."

"You think they'll like our music?"

"Miss Daisy, anyone who doesn't like your music is already dead."

They all laughed.

They worked out the numbers, and Daisy insisted that everything be split 3 ways but that Boyd get 5 percent. "After all, if it weren't for him, we'd never exist."

"What about 3 percent — and you come back home whenever you're tired of traveling," Boyd suggested.

"Done," Daisy, Matthew, Thomas, and Pettyjohn all said together.

"I'll draw up the papers," Pettyjohn said as they all stood to go.

Daisy stepped over to Boyd and looked up to him. "Did you talk to Juana Bell again?"

"Not since the other day when we were all together. Why?"

"She's decided to stay with Dr. Askew. And it could be for more than being a nurse."

THE END

Thanks

Thank you for taking the time to read The Hussy and the Hardcase. I hope you enjoyed it. If you did, please consider posting a short review on line at the site where you purchased the book and telling your friends. Word of mouth is an author's best friend and much appreciated. I love to write these stories, but it's even better to sell some and to know other people take some joy from them, too.

If you're interested is subscribing to my monthly newsletter, contact me at jacks@wrightbridgepress.com. You know when my next novel is coming out and a little bit about how I work. I would love to hear from you.

Thank you,
    Jack R. Stanley

BONUS

***

6 Chapter of

THE GAVEL AND THE GUN
Vol. 1

CHAPTER ONE

Three cowboys sat on the ground around a small fire in a steady drizzle.

"Hello, the camp!" a call came from out of the dark.

All three cowboys leap to their feet with their pistols in their hands.

"Who's there?" the eldest man of 30 with a full and bushy beard yelled back.

"A pilgrim on his way home to Texas," came the response. "For a place at your fire, I'll share my coffee and some beans!"

"Come in slowly," the cowboy leader said after exchanging looks with his fellow riders. "Gun belt over your saddle horn and your hands in the open."

"I'm unarmed — but I'll come easy."

The rider approached slowly on a tired-looking roan. He held his reins high in one hand and the other hand away from his body, fingers spread.

"How come you ain't armed?" the lead cowboy said suspiciously.

"I'm a circuit-riding preacher. Spent the winter up in Kansas with a trail drive — but I'm headed home now."

The rider stopped in the dim light of the hissing fire. His hat

THE HUSSY AND THE HARDCASE

drooped on all sides, and his slicker covered most of his body. He looked up into the sky, saying, "The Lord sends the rains on the just and the unjust."

"Amen," said one of the cowboys putting his six-gun away.

"I am grateful but wet and tired," the rider said. "Still, what I have I am willing to share."

"Then climb on down and pull up a rock," the second cowboy said, putting his pistol back in its holster. "We're headed south, too. Hopin' t' make Texas tomorrow."

"We're back from trailin' longhorns up to Sedalia."

"If you could stand the company," the preacher said, "I'd take it as a kindness to ride along with you."

"You're welcome," the bearded cowboy said, lowering his pistol but not holstering it. "Climb down and come get yourself warm."

"Bless you, friend," the preacher said as he angled his roan, so it was between him and the cowboys as he dismounted. "But I promised coffee -- and I got a few beans," he said, reaching into his saddlebags.

As the preacher placed a hand on his horse's rump and walked around the animal, he appeared with .45 Colt in his hand. Without another word, he shot the bearded leader who still held his pistol at his side in the center of his chest. Before the other men could react, he turned and repeated his deadly aim on the other two men, throwing them backward to mud puddles.

The camp was silent for a moment as the *"preacher"* tipped back his hat to reveal a nasty scar across one eye and down his right cheek.

"They're all dead, boys!" he called into the night. Two rough-looking men rode in wearing slickers.

"Ace, you get the horses," their leader ordered. "Will and I will check t' see if these fellow's left anything worthwhile for us."

The pair dismounted. Ace, the skinny hook-nosed one, held his gun in his hand as he made his way to the hobbled horses.

"There's four horses here, Rosco!"

"And there are four saddles on the ground," added the other standing near the fire. This one pulled his pistol. "And one of these men is still alive."

"You know what to do, Will," Rosco said.

Will fired twice. "*Was alive*," he said.

"Bring the horses and throw saddles on each one. If there's another cowboy out there, we'll kill him, too, if need be!" the "preacher," Rosco, said loud enough to be heard anywhere nearby.

The one called Ace brought the horses down to the fire. The thin framed man glanced at the dead cowboys on the ground.

"When you kill a man, Rosco, make sure he's dead 'fore you walk away." Shaggy headed Will Hoxie pulled his holstered revolver and fired once. He hit one of the dead cowboys in the head. "Now, that's the way it's done."

The three killers mounted up and rode out, leading the four riderless horses.

Back in the rocks, a 17-year-old cowboy named, Dell, watched with his black-powder pistol in his hand but was too scared to make a sound.

Fifty-one-year-old Ottis Vanderhoff showed his age, the ravages of being on the losing side in the war, and trying to hack out a life as a half-breed farming in the Indian Territory. He could still do a full day's plowing in the field he had left fallow last year when he turned his mule, Ruff, around and started another row. Three black men stepped out from behind a bush as Ottis pulled up on the reins and faced the three.

"Uziel," Ottis said, addressing the group's leader. All were obvious former slaves, but Uziel was a big lazy man. "Thought you said you'd never set foot on this land again. You back looking for work?"

"I ain't your slave no more, Ottis," the angry man spat out.

"No," said Ottis, "but I have no more to offer you now than I had before — food and a roof over your head. We've got no money. We're just tryin' t' stay alive. And there's only enough work for one -- not you and your friends."

"I ain't come t' beggin'."

"Never thought you did."

"You owe me. You owe all of us!"

THE HUSSY AND THE HARDCASE

"I was always fair to you, Uziel. You ate what we ate and had as good a shelter as we had."

"But I slept in the barn!"

"I have nothing more t' offer you now." Ottis looked at Uziel's two partners. "We can offer your friends a meal — but there's not enough work for them."

"We didn't come to work," Uziel said, glancing at each of his partners.

"This is a dry land farm. That's all there is. If you don't want t' work — I've got nothing for you."

Ottis turned back to his mule and popped the reins.

Uziel leaned down and picked up a flat rock. With a vicious blow, he smashed it into the back of Ottis's head, breaking bone and splattering blood into the dust. Ottis was dead before his knees hit the furrows.

Inside the farmhouse, a full-blooded Choctaw woman, Lutie, Ottis's wife, was baking an apple pie when she heard heavy footsteps on the back porch.

"Who gave out first? Ruff or you, Ottis?" she joked as she wiped her hands on her apron. "And don't you even think of trackin' those dirty boots into my kitchen."

When she looked up, she saw the big black man standing there with two others behind him.

"Uziel? I thought once you got your freedom, we'd never see you around these parts again?"

She approached him, looking around his huge frame.

"Where's Ottis? You should have seen him out in the north field."

"He ain't there no more," Uziel said with a slightly cruel smile.

"Where is he?" Lutie asked, pushing him aside and stepping outside.

"Same place you goin'," he said, bringing a hatchet down and splitting her skull open. "T' hell!"

The woman fell to the planks and didn't move.

Uziel's friends stepped over her body, and the three men went inside the house.

★★★

"Come on, Bart! You're almost there!"

Tollie worked hard at her job, and she was good at it. She was the best whore in Muskogee Maude's "Big House" for almost five years since her husband, a clerk, had been killed in a bank robbery there. This was the only job she could get that would keep her and her son, Bobby, fed, clothed, and a roof over their heads. She had grown up in an orphanage and was willing to do anything to keep her child from knowing that same fate.

Bart Zolan was an overweight, mid-40's, hairy lump of a man — too drunk to focus on what he was doing. Finally, Tollie stopped and climbed off of him.

"Do you want to try again in a minute — when you're rested up?"

"Hell, no!" he said, reaching for the bottle on the bedside table.

Tollie wrapped herself in the top sheet and went to the dresser to wash up.

"Come on, Bart. I'm tryin' my best here."

"I don't give a damn. You're just a whore to me."

"Damn you, Bart Zolan!" she said, turning on him. "This ain't the first time you've quit on me. You don't finish, I don't get paid." She dropped the sheet. "Let's try again!"

"Then here's your pay, bitch!" He grabbed his .44 Remington out of his holster hanging on the bedpost, pulled back the hammer and shot Tollie between her breasts.

The room rang with the thunder of the blast inside the closed space. But a few moments later, there were footsteps on the upstairs hallway outside the door. Men carrying pistols and Henry repeating rifles, in long johns and Levi's, all without boots, gathered near the door.

"It came from in here," one voice said as Zolan shoved his feet into his boots and buckled his belt. Bart fired two shots through the door before snatching up his dirty shirt and climbing out the window and onto the balcony. He was over the rail and sliding down a pole when a rifle shot splintered the door jam and armed men rushed in.

All they found was young Tollie dead, the window curtains moving in the breeze through the open window, and a vest hanging on a chair with the U.S. Marshal's badge still pinned to it.

A dozen riders holding burning torches against the darkness, their heads covered with flour or seed sacks with a pair of eye holes cut in each, led a single circled rider with his hands bound behind him. This gagged rider was missing one leg from the left knee down. He wore a Confederate Army cap and almost worn out gray rebel Army pants.

The group stopped under a tall tree that had a thick branch extended across the dusty road. One of the hooded men tossed a rope over the branch while another dismounted and swung the end of the line around the base of the tree, ready to tie it off.

Another hooded rider untied the gag.

The guest of this neck-tie party spoke to the other party-goers.

"You can't hang me! I didn't do nothing! I showed you the bill of sale for this horse! I bought and paid for him!"

The leader of the vigilantes rode over and showed the bound man a sheet of paper.

"Yeah," the victim said, "that's it! You can keep the horse."

The leader folded and stuffed the bill of sale into the bound man's pocket while another removed the rebel cap and slipped a loop over his head.

"Hey, that's not even a proper hangman's knot. That will choke me to death!"

Once the loop was secured and tightened around the victim's scruffy neck, the rider at the foot of the tree tied off the rope. The line was tight and rubbed against the man's throat as he sat up in the saddle.

"This ain't right!" the suspected horse thief said. "What kind of men are you to hang an innocent man without a trial?"

The vigilantes backed their horses up away from the man in the saddle with the rope around his neck. Then slowly, they walked their mounts back the way they came. It was only after they were away from the tree that the riders urged their horses into trots and then gallops.

The bound man was left alone with the rope over the branch and tied to the tree sitting on his mount.

"Cowards!" he shouts, and his horse starts to move. "Whoa, girl," he says gently to the horse.

The man sat there as the vigilantes rode away, and he was left in the silent night, knowing he would live only so long as his horse remained still.

CHAPTER TWO

The stern-wheeler Queen of the City tied up at the docks in Ft. Smith. Sitting on the dock on a bale of cotton waiting to be loaded aboard was a balding man holding a bowler hat in his ink-stained hands. He had mutton chops and two days' growth of beard on his 40 year-old-face. He peered over his wire-rimmed glasses at the first passenger to come down the gangplank.

It was a big man, 6' 5" in black military boots, blue pants, and a cavalry hat without any insignia. With deep blue eyes, auburn hair, and a square jaw, the man looked confident and had an air of authority about him. But he was not threatening even though he wore a big flap covered revolver in a cross draw holster on the front edge of his left hip.

"Welcome to Ft. Smith," said the man stepping down from the cotton bale and extending a hand. "Claxton Landers," he said, "reporter, editor, owner of *the* Ft. Smith Daily Ledger."

"Mr. Landers," the tall man said. "Mace Truax. Pleased to meet you."

"New people in town are news," Lander said, producing a folded piece of paper and a pencil. "Mind if I as you a couple of questions."

"Nope," Truax said.

"What brings you to our fair frontier town?"

"I'm low on funds. And have a desire to continue to eat."

The newspaperman laughed.

"I do understand that, Mr. Truax," he scribbled a note on his piece of paper. "You're late of the cavalry unless I miss my guess. I say -- an officer?"

"That I am -- or was. But the Army's got more captains these days than it needs. I've been killing Indians since before the war in Texas -- and then out West with the Army. They're like ants and flies. You can't kill 'em all. I decided it was time for me to move on to something else."

"Anything in particular?"

"At the moment, I'm looking for an honest poker game. My poke could use a little refreshing."

"Try The Sidewheeler -- center of town. You can't miss it. They don't put up with slick gamblers."

"I'll do that." Truax tipped his hat, "Mr. Landers."

"Thanks for your time, Mr. Truax."

Another man, squat, sweat-stained shirt, and green eye-shade on his thinning hair, hurried up out of breath. He was in his early 50's and wore a sour expression.

"Who was that?" he panted, watching Truax walk up the hill.

"You can read about him in tomorrow's edition," Claxton said.

"Bastard."

"Pick, if you had gotten here first, would you have told me?"

"Go t' hell, Claxton."

The editor laughs and says, "He's a fellow just out of the Army looking for a poker game to make some money."

"No carpetbagger judge, yet?"

"Is that the way he'll be characterized in The Vindicator?"

"We report the truth."

"Or at least your version of it."

"There he is," the older man said, pointing up to a passenger without a hat. "See, carpetbagger."

The man stepping down the stairs from the stateroom to the main deck was average height, a full head of dark brown hair, a mustache and goatee. He wore a black three-piece suit, and in his hand, he carried a round handled walking cane and carpetbag.

"Made up your mind already have you, Pick," Claxton said. "Give the man a chance. He can't be worse than Judge Story. Even you called him corrupt."

"Story's gone, and this jasper is who we'll have to deal with now."

"Might not be a bad idea to start out on his good side."

"He's a Yankee. That's enough for me."

"The war's been over for 10 years, Pick. Even you should be reconstructed by now."

"Never!" the older man said. "He was a Lincoln Republican -- and Grant appointed him judge. Yankee."

★★★

The new judge shook hands with the steamboat captain who tipped his hat, and the judge stepped down the gangplank.

"Judge," Claxton called, but the jurist didn't respond. The editor tried again, "Judge Issac Parker!"

Parker looked up at Claxton.

"You'll have to excuse me. I'm not used to the title quite yet."

"I'm Claxton Landers -- editor of the Ft. Smith Daily Ledger."

The Judge shook hands with Claxton.

"My pleasure to meet you, Mr. Claxton."

"This is my competitor, Mr. Joseph Pickering, editor of The Vindicator."

"I can speak for myself," Pick says.

"Good afternoon, gentlemen. What can I do for you?"

"You're Grant's Yankee judge, right?" Pickering asked with a sneer.

"I am the new Federal Judge for the Western District of Arkansas -- appointed by President Grant and confirmed by the Senate -- as are all Federal judges. As for being a Yankee -- no, I consider myself an American."

"And what are your plans for Ft. Smith and the Indian Territory?" Claxton cut in.

"I intend to bring justice and fairness to everyone in this jurisdiction."

"Judge, there's a popular saying -- 'There's no Sunday West of St. Louis -- and no God West of Ft. Smith.'"

"Perhaps that was true in the past -- but this is a new day."

"You believe one man can make a difference?" Pickering jabbed his short pencil at the judge.

"Judas Iscariot was one man, Mr. Pickering, but so was Simon Peter. Of course, one man can make a difference. And a tree is known by the fruits it bears. I hope to be judged by my actions."

"What about your marshal?"

"A mister -- Zolan, I believe? What about him?"

"Your honor," Claxton interrupted Pick's questioning, "there's evidence he shot and murdered a young woman in Muskogee -- over in the Territory."

"A whore," Pick added. "He got away, but he left his badge behind."

"I'll issue a warrant for Mr. Zolon's arrest."

"You won't find any deputies ready to take up that warrant."

"Then, I'll appoint a new marshal who will."

"You are ambitious, I'll give you that, Judge," Pickering said.

CHAPTER THREE

A carriage pulled up, driven by a man in his late 30's, short, thin, blond-haired, wearing a suit. The man climbed down, removing his bowler hat.

"Judge Issac Parker?" he asked.

"Yes," the judge answered.

"Sir, I am a Presley Cross, your court clerk. I apologize for my tardiness. The stable owner didn't have the carriage ready when he had promised."

"I appreciate you coming to get me, Mr. Cross."

"I'll see to your luggage, Your Honor."

"Thank you, sir," the judge said as Cross hurried up the gangplank.

"This man Zolan," the judge continued to the two reporters/editors, "is to be considered innocent until proven guilty. That's the way everyone charged with a crime will be treated in this court."

"That is if he ever gets to court," Pickering said.

"He will, Mr. Pickering. My goal is swift and honest justice."

"Hell, Judge, there hasn't been a trial here in two years."

"We don't even have a district attorney to prosecute cases," Claxton said.

"It seems I have a lot of work to do."

CHAPTER THREE

Cross returned leading two men who carried trunks and bags which they deposited in the carriage.

"I have secured you a room at our best hotel, Your Honor. We can deliver your belonging there, and then I can show you the court if you like."

"Very much, Mr. Cross. Thank you for your efficiency and attention to detail."

Cross didn't appear to know how to respond to these compliments.

The judge climbed up in the seat beside Cross.

"Can I offer you gentlemen a ride to town?" the judge asked the reporters.

"Not me," Pickering said.

"Thank you, no, Your Honor. There are other places I need to visit to see about news. We appreciate the offer."

"I"m sure I'll be seeing you both again soon," the judge said, nodding his head.

As Cross drove the wagon, Judge Parker got his first look at the frontier town. The main street was wide but certainly not paved. Rutted and dusty, it was typical of western towns. There were two banks, and there were several merchant buildings, wholesales shops, shippers, and an abundance of saloons.

"Tell me about Bart Zolan," he said, looking around at the buildings and the people.

"A bully and a braggart. He liked his authority, and he liked to hurt people. To your predecessor, Zolan was a good marshal."

"He's certainly not the kind of man I want in the job."

After a moment, the Judge asked, "How many deputy marshals do we have."

"We are allotted two hundred but we have never had more than half of that on the payroll."

"Is it true then none will pick up the warrant on Zolan?"

"No warrant has been issued. Based on witness statements, one of the deputy marshals's collected, I've drawn it up, but it awaits your signature."

"We'll go to the office shortly, and I'll sign it." They rode on a moment more before the Judge said, "Tell me about these marshals."

CHAPTER THREE

"A deputy is paid $150 plus $2 per live prisoner he brings in -- 6 cents a mile for travel and he has to pay to feed his prisoners and must pay for the burial of any he kills."

"None of them wants the warrant for Zolan. I've asked. Whoever takes that job will have to be willing to go after Zolan himself."

They passed the Sidewheeler Saloon, a liquor and card palace, which was maybe a little cleaner looking than the average Western saloon.

"At the Sidewheeler -- there -- tonight. Every attorney in town will be there.

"For what?"

"A reception -- to welcome you, Your Honor."

"Good. I'll see what I can do about lining up a persecutor.

After some of the judge's bags were unloaded at the hotel Le Flore, Mr. Cross was ready to take his passenger to the courthouse. However, before they could move, a barred wagon with five prisoners in it passed by.

"Where are they going?" the judge asked.

"To the jail. It's attached to the courthouse, Your Honor."

A lawman rode a dappled gray gelding behind the wagon. He wore buckskin pants and a faded cotton shirt and no hat.

"Is there a deputy who you'd recommend for the Marshal's job?"

"Heck Thomas -- but he's out serving warrants. Could be a month or more before he returns."

"I don't think we can wait that long. Who is that deputy?" the judge motioned toward the retreating rider with the wagon load of prisoners.

"He's not a deputy. That's John Browneagle -- Indian Police -- Choctaw Lighthorse in his case."

John Browneagle was not an imposing man, just over 5 feet 8 inches tall, with straight black hair and deeply tanned skin. But there was something confident about the way he carried himself.

"Lighthouse?"

CHAPTER THREE

"That's what the Indian Police force is called He operates somewhat under your jurisdiction, but he's the Indian Agent for his tribe."

"Somewhat?"

"He works for the Five Civilized Tribes. But Browneagle is one of the best."

"I want to see the jail."

"Before you do, Your Honor, there's one more thing I'd like to show you."

"Lead on, Mr. Cross."

The carriage headed down the street and out of town.

"Where I'm taking you, Your Honor, is a place called The Hanging Tree. It's been used by vigilantes in these parts for years."

"There will be no more of that, I assure you, Mr. Cross. Vigilante justice is no justice."

"It's better than nothing -- sometimes better than the justice coming out of the courthouse. I'm speaking of your predecessor."

"We must send a strong message, Mr. Cross -- and quickly that there is justice here -- as well as law and order."

The two rode on in silence until the judge turned to his clerk.

"Mr. Cross, there's something stuck in your craw. I would be obliged if you'd spit it out. If we're going to be working together, I think frankness should be the order of the day -- every day."

"Well, for one thing, we're *not* going to be working together."

"I beg your pardon?"

"I've been the clerk for this court for eight years and under three different judges. One is now a territorial governor, one is in Congress, and the last was this close to being put on trial himself. What I've seen I would not call law, order, or justice."

"Go on."

"I am very aware of what your new position pays, and it is hardly what I'd call the job of a lifetime from someone who'd studied the law and who had the influence to obtain such an appointment. It's a stepping stone -- a short stop along the way for someone who has greater ambitions -- not an end unto itself."

"I assure you, Mr. Cross, you'd be surprised how little *influence* it required. There wasn't a line of applicants for this position."

CHAPTER THREE

"I happen to be a man of principals, Your Honor -- principals which I believe surpassed those of anyone I've seen on this bench. I was a school teacher but choose to take the job of court clerk because I hoped to make a difference. I love the country and the people I've gotten to know here -- but I can make more of a difference in a classroom than I can in the courthouse."

"Then why have you stayed so long?"

"Hope. I have hoped against all the evidence I've seen that a jurist will ascend to this court and make some real changes. I'm no quitter, but as soon as you are settled into your job, I will be leaving."

"That sounds very noble, Mr. Cross, but it appears to me that *quitting* is exactly what you are doing. I'm not here on my way to anywhere else. I came to Ft. Smith and to this court to dispense justice. Your help is appreciated for as long as you decide to stay, but please don't pass judgment on me based on what you've seen in the past."

The carriage rounded a curve on the wooded road, and Cross pulled the horses to a halt. Ahead of them sat a man astride a horse with a rope around his neck.

CHAPTER FOUR

"Whoa -- back, girl," the lean man on the horse croaked out as he used his one good leg and his wooden peg to urge the animal to back up.

"Slowly," the Judge said to his driver as the two men stepped down to the ground.

"Please..." the man with a rope burned neck whispered as loudly as he can.

"Go cut the rope at the base of the tree," the Judge said as he approached the horse.

"I have nothing to cut it with," Cross said.

The Judge pulled a pocket knife out of one vest pocket and unhooked it from the gold chain, which connected it to the watch in his other pocket. He tossed the knife to Cross, who caught it and opened the blade.

"Steady," the judge said to the horse as he approached. The animal stepped back and strained the rope in the other direction. Judge Parker stopped, and so did the horse.

Cross reached the tree and began sawing through the threads of the rope, but it was not going very fast.

"Remind me to keep that knife sharpened, Mr. Cross."

The horse shook its head and snorted as the Judge began to move again.

"Whoa," the desperate man squeaked out.

Suddenly the horse bolted, and the judge rushed forward and grabbed the man by the legs as he slipped from the saddle. Cross kept sawing and finally got through the rope. The hanged man's full weight fell on the Judge, who then eased him to the ground.

The man gasped for air as the judge removed the rope.

"Do we have a canteen?"

"There's one on the horse."

"Get it."

For some reason, the frightened horse allowed Cross to approach and take the canteen off the saddle horn. The clerk patted the animal and quickly brought the water to the judge and the victim now on the ground.

The man drank several gulps from the canteen.

"Do you know who he is?" Judge Parker asked Cross.

"His name is Stonewall Welch. Hard case -- former Confederate. See, he still wears part of the uniform." Cross looked around. "Usually he wears the cap, too. They call him 'Stoney.'"

"Lost my leg at Chickamauga," the exhausted man rasps with pride. "We sure kicked the Yankee's ass that day."

"Who was trying to hang you?" the judge asked.

"Didn't introduce themselves," Stoney Welch managed to say.

"Why did they do this to you?"

"Stealin' my horse. But I got the bill of sale in my pocket."

"There was a shooting in one of the local saloons two nights ago," Cross said. "This man killed a gambler named Tom Bartlett."

"Crooked gambler. And a fair fight. He drew on me."

"Bartlett did have a less than stellar reputation."

"Damn straight."

"As to who drew first -- there are differing opinions on that."

"Then I'm placing you under arrest, Mr. Welch," the judge said, helping Stoney to his feet.

"Arrest? Fer what? I'm th' one's almost hung."

"Manslaughter -- perhaps even murder. We'll have to see."

"Who the hell are you?"

"I'm Judge Issac Parker."

"The new District Court Judge," Cross added.

"Don't worry, you'll get a fair trial, that I can guarantee."

"And then you'll hang me -- again?"

"If you're found guilty."

"I ain't guilty. I told you the son of a bitch drew on me."

"That's for a jury to decide. Get yourself a lawyer."

"Lawyer? With what? Them vigilantes took all the money I had left."

"Then, the court will see to it that you have an adequate defense."

"Adequate? Hell, I need a miracle! Half th' men in this town are Yankees!"

"The war is over, Mr. Welch."

"Not for me."

"It will be if you're hanged," Cross said.

The jail had three levels. Connected to the old barracks building, which served as the courthouse, the two-story brick building sat on a whitewashed stone foundation and basement. All windows were barred, and a slanted walkway led from ground level down to the jail's lower level.

Judge Parker and Mr. Cross ushered Stoney Welch down the ramp to the jail where they were met by Herb Irwin, jailer, and chief guard. The pale-skinned, overweight, hulking man with beady eyes took the new prisoner and led him to a cell.

"This place stinks," Judge Parker said, wrinkling his face.

"It'll get worse as the summer drags on," Cross told him.

When Herb Irwin returned, Judge Parker said, "Mr. Irwin, I want you to clean this place up. There is no reason for this stench."

"It's a jail, Judge. It ain't supposed to be a hotel."

"And each man here is innocent until proven guilty. Clean it up!"

The courthouse was an old two-story, converted military barracks, perhaps it had been a former headquarters at some point. It had a porch, several windows, and an overall official look about it. But the building was in disrepair. Spokes were missing from the porch and stair railings. Weeds also thrived around the plank front steps.

Judge Parker and Presley Cross mounted the stairs, stepped across the porch, and pushed open the double front door. A set of stairs led to the upper floor. On this floor, though, there was an anti room, and beyond that, an empty courtroom with benches for observers, a dozen chairs for the jury, and at the rear of the space, a dust-covered judge's bench.

The Judge walked down the center aisle of the room and paused to wipe his hand across the railing that separated the gallery from the rest of the court. He looked at his hand. It was dusty. He threw a disapproving glance at Cross.

"There didn't seem to be much point in keeping it clean. The place was never used -- like I said -- for two years."

Judge Parker shook his head and walked across to look at the jury box, scanning the empty chairs from one end to the other.

"That's another problem," Cross said. "The juries. It reached a point where they were never paid -- or if they were -- it was as much as a year later."

The Judge turned to face Cross.

"I have some money, Mr. Cross. I want you to set up an account with the biggest local bank. Pay the jurors out of that -- reimburse me when Washington finally gets around to it."

"You might want to think that over, Your Honor."

"There's nothing to think about. We will have no court unless we have juries -- jury service is a civic duty, but jurors deserve to be paid for their time."

Cross shrugged. "Whatever you say." He made himself a note.

The Judge crossed over and examined the judge's bench and chair. It, too, was dusty and held a neglected gavel. Cross moved over to the door behind the bench, which led out of the courtroom to a back staircase.

"The offices are up this way."

The Judge crossed to the door and followed Mr. Cross up the stairs.

CHAPTER FIVE

"This will do very nicely," Judge Parker said, examining what would be his office. There were a large desk and padded high back chair, two windows, a work table, wall to wall bookcases, all empty at the moment, and two visitor chairs near a fireplace.

"Your books will be delivered tomorrow," Cross said. "I talked to the steamboat's captain."

The sound of footsteps was heard coming up another staircase. Cross went through the door to his adjoining office and opened the outer door. The judge continued to look around his space.

A figure stopped in the judge's door and then turned back to Cross. At first glance, it was difficult to tell if this visitor was male or female. On a second look, it became evident that it was a woman. She was dressed in men's clothes, and while somewhat attractive, she was dirty. The woman was in her early 30's.

She spoke to Cross, who stood behind the door he had opened to allow her in.

"There you are, you little weasel," she stepped over to Cross and shook her finger in his face. "You *told* me he'd be in today -- and --." She stopped and whipped around on the Judge again. "You that there new judge?"

CHAPTER FIVE

The woman had an attractive figure, even her clothes couldn't hide. Her hair, which needed a good wash and combing was black as her eyes.

The Judge found this woman interesting. He stepped across his office to her.

"I am. Judge Isaac Parker. I'm afraid you have the advantage of me, madam. Who are you?"

She let out a deep belly laugh. She was still laughing when she managed to speak. "I've worked in a couple of houses -- but I ain't no *madam*."

"I beg your pardon. I meant the term as one of respect, not of derision."

"*Derision?* Damn, but you must be a judge usin' words like that." She extended a small calloused hand to the judge. "I'm Bell Starr."

"Is it Miss — or Mrs?"

Starting to laugh again, she said, "Hell, honey, it's jest Bell."

They shook hands.

"Bell," the judge said after a moment, "is there something I can do for you?"

"Damn right there is. Get Uriah Starr out of your hoosegow."

The judge didn't grasp what she was saying. He turned to Cross standing behind Bell in his office.

"Uriah Starr -- this woman's -- common-law husband -- and...."

"He's my husband -- all legal as can be"

Judge Parker reacted to this in surprise but focused on Cross to make it clear.

"Husband -- then?"

"I don't give a damn what ya' call 'im, I jest want t' get him out."

"What are the charges against this -- Uriah Starr?"

"The same as always -- bootlegging."

Bell spoke up again, "Tell your judge about my -- whatever you call that thing Temple Houston fixed up for me?"

Cross was displeased with this, but he sighed and explained.

"Mr. Temple Houston -- whom you will meet tonight -- drew up a writ of habeas corpus. It seems all the evidence against Mr. Starr -- *mysteriously* -- disappeared."

"Ya' might say it was magic. But that's nobody's ne nothin' t' prove he done nothin'. So you got no right t up in that damn 'stink hole down there."

"I've been telling her that no one could act or new judge."

Bell turned to the judge.

"S' you're th' new judge -- and you're here an' so am I. Now let's get Uriah out."

"Would you please give the man a chance. He hasn't been in town a full day, yet. Tomorrow will be soon enough."

"Th' hell, it will!" Bell bellowed.

Judge Parker said, "Mr. Cross. Let me see the writ, please."

Cross made a face, glared at Bell, and then turned to his desk.

Judge Parker motioned to one of the visitor chairs.

"I'm afraid everything is little dusty -- Bell --but have a seat."

"Hell, I don't mind a little dirt."

She sat, leaning forward, her elbows on her knees like a man. She watched the judge as he went around behind his desk, pulled out a pair of glasses, and cleaned them with his handkerchief.

After a moment, Bell spook again.

"Talk is you're an Indian lover, nigger-lover, and you're a carpetbagger."

The judge stopped cleaning his glasses and looked up at Bell.

Bell threw her hands up.

"Hey -- I don't give a damn. I had a brother killed by the rebs -- my first husband was a damn Yankee. They shot him fer desertin'. I was raised by a mammy who was black as th' ace a' spades -- an' th' man I'm livin' with -- Uriah -- he's part Shawnee. I'm jest tellin' you what people are sayin'."

Cross stepped back into the judge's office carrying a two-page legal brief. He went over to the judge and handed him the pages. The judge accepted the brief, he put on his glasses and read the document quickly as Cross gave Bell a dirty look.

After a couple of moments, Judge Parker looked up and took a second look at the top of the document.

"Temple Houston. Sam Houston's son? He practices in Ft. Smith?"

CHAPTER FIVE

"Ya' might say it was magic. But that's nobody's never mind. Ya' got nothin' t' prove he done nothin'. So you got no right t' keep him locked up in that damn 'stink hole down there."

"I've been telling her that no one could act on this -- except the new judge."

Bell turned to the judge.

"S' you're th' new judge -- and you're here an' so am I. Now let's get Uriah out."

"Would you please give the man a chance. He hasn't been in town a full day, yet. Tomorrow will be soon enough."

"Th' hell, it will!" Bell bellowed.

Judge Parker said, "Mr. Cross. Let me see the writ, please."

Cross made a face, glared at Bell, and then turned to his desk.

Judge Parker motioned to one of the visitor chairs.

"I'm afraid everything is little dusty -- Bell --but have a seat."

"Hell, I don't mind a little dirt."

She sat, leaning forward, her elbows on her knees like a man. She watched the judge as he went around behind his desk, pulled out a pair of glasses, and cleaned them with his handkerchief.

After a moment, Bell spook again.

"Talk is you're an Indian lover, nigger-lover, and you're a carpetbagger."

The judge stopped cleaning his glasses and looked up at Bell.

Bell threw her hands up.

"Hey -- I don't give a damn. I had a brother killed by the rebs -- my first husband was a damn Yankee. They shot him fer desertin'. I was raised by a mammy who was black as th' ace a' spades -- an' th' man I'm livin' with -- Uriah -- he's part Shawnee. I'm jest tellin' you what people are sayin'."

Cross stepped back into the judge's office carrying a two-page legal brief. He went over to the judge and handed him the pages. The judge accepted the brief, he put on his glasses and read the document quickly as Cross gave Bell a dirty look.

After a couple of moments, Judge Parker looked up and took a second look at the top of the document.

"Temple Houston. Sam Houston's son? He practices in Ft. Smith?"

CHAPTER FIVE

"Mr. Cross, is there something you'd like to say. I don't believe we finished our conversation in the buggy."

"Your Honor, I happen to be a man of principle."

"Yes, you told me that."

"Is what just happened the kind of justice you plan to dispense -- allowing the likes of Uriah Starr to go free?"

"Justice, Mr. Cross, is blind. She treats all men the same. There was no evidence with which to try Mr. Starr -- be he innocent or guilty. Without it, he does not deserve to be in jail."

"This kind of thing will make you very popular with certain elements in these parts."

"I did not come here to be popular. Neither, as I told you before, did I come here expecting to step from this position to another political post. What if it had been you instead of Mr. Starr in jail and no evidence. How long would you feel it just to keep you incarcerated?"

There was a silence between the judge and his clerk.

"Mr. Cross, your knowledge and assistance are greatly appreciated -- for however long you decide to remain in your job. But don't you take your toys and run home blaming anyone but yourself if it takes longer than it should to get things straightened out. If you are interested in justice, I suggest you button up your courage and get back to work. Court opens at 8 o'clock tomorrow morning -- and I expect this place to be clean."

The judge crossed to the door with Cross watching -- the clerk's mouth open but no word forthcoming. The judge stopped before he left.

"Please call for me at my hotel -- if you are still disposed to introduce me to the town's attorneys tonight. If not, I'll find my own way."

The judge walked out, leaving Cross in the empty offices when he encountered a young cowboy, hat in hand outside in the hall at the Marshal's closed door.

"Can I help you?" Parker asked.

"I was lookin' fer th' Marshal."

"I'm afraid we don't have one at the moment. What do you need?"

Mr. Cross heard the conversation and stepped out behind the judge

CHAPTER FIVE

as the young man said, "My name's Dell -- Dell Maguire. I'm a cowboy from Texas."

"All right," the judge said, trying to be patient. "Why did you need to see the Marshal?"

"The three men I was ridin' with --," he swallowed before finishing, "-- they was murdered in our camp -- about a week back. It's taken me this long to get here afoot."

"Do you know who killed them?"

"I heard them use the names -- Rosco, Ace -- and Will."

"Could be Rosco Dury," Cross said as he stepped forward. "He calls himself 'preacher' sometimes."

"That's what they called him," the young cowboy said.

"He rides with Ace Keogh and Will Hoxie," the clerk offered.

"Could you identify these men if you saw them again?" the judge asked.

Dell nodded his head and tightened his jaw. "I'll never forget them faces."

CHAPTER SIX

The editor of the Ft. Smith Daily Ledger, Claxton Landers, stood at the bar in his rumpled suit, enjoying a beer with a merchant in a business suit. The businessman finished his drink, shook hands with Claxton, and left. Claxton tilted back his bowler hat and turned to the activity in the saloon.

From one of the side rooms, Mace Truax, the first passenger to emerge from the Queen of the City riverboat that morning, stepped out pocketing a wad of greenbacks. The tall, former army officer went to the bar and took up a position beside the newspaperman.

"Captain Truax," Claxton began stroking his mutton chops, "I see you found your poker game."

"That I did," the former soldier said in his deep voice. "And did all right -- for a while."

"Let me guess. You met a man in a white suit and hat -- a mustache. Then your luck seems to change."

"How'd you figure that?"

"Oh, I've seen it happen before. I'm thinking you were smart enough to get out while you were still ahead."

"Let's say I got out while the gettin' was good."

Claxton Landers chuckles. "Not everyone is so wise."

CHAPTER SIX

"Three or four hours ago, I was doin' pretty well. Then that fella' showed up."

"Figure he's cheating'?"

"If he is, I'll be damned if I can see how."

"He's not. You just met Temple Houston."

"Sam Houston's son?"

"That's him."

"Hmmm. I use t' work for his ol' man, Governor Sam."

"How's that?"

"I was a Texas Ranger 'til the war was over. I was on the Texas Indian frontier."

"Let me buy you a drink," Claxton said.

"I can pay for my own, now," Mace said.

"It's a gesture of friendship."

"Accepted."

"Jules!" he called the bartender. To Mace, he said, "What's your pleasure?

"A beer would suit my pistol just fine."

"Two beers."

"Comin' up." the sandy-haired barkeep said.

When the brews arrived, Claxton proposed a toast. "To you, Captain."

"Make it, Mace. I'm shut of the Army for good."

"To you, Mace Truax."

"And to you, Mr. Landers."

"Claxton."

"Claxton."

They drank.

"I'll tell you something," the editor said, setting the beer down. "Temple Houston doesn't cheat. Doesn't have to. He's simply that good at reading other people."

"Well, he read me well enough."

"Mace -- I've seen Houston win $5,000 at that table in one night."

"Five thousand?"

"And when the game was over, he told the other man what his *tell* was. The man agreed and left without a word. The next night Houston was back and lost it all -- and then some."

"You don't say."

"Made a believer out of me -- at that same table, once. Cleaned me out. Told me, 'Don't bet it if you can't afford to lose.'"

"That's been my rule," the larger man said.

"So you goin' back to Texas?"

"Oh, I don't know. Stories I've heard about Texas since the war don't sound all that inviting, t' me.

Just then, the sound of shattering bar glasses came from behind Claxton. He and Mace turned.

Two cowboy types, dirty, rough, big, and over half-drunk, Dutch and Coy, had squared off at each other a few feet away from the bar. Dutch, the larger of the two, had a big bowie knife in his hand, ready to slash Coy, who had pulled his cap and ball pistol.

"I'm goin' t' gut you, Coy. Slit you open like the hog you are!

"Like hell you are, you lying' piece of shit! I'm goin' t' blow your fool head off -- leave your ears with nothin' t' hang on to!"

Judge Parker and Mr. Cross, both clean and in fresh clothes, stepped into the saloon and stood watching by the front doors. Everyone else in the place was also focused on the two drunks.

"You ain't goin' t' do nothin'!" Coy declared.

"Oh, yeah, Dutch?!!"

Coy, swayed in his tracks, used both his thumbs to pull back the hammer of his weapon.

But before Coy could pull the trigger, Mace pulled his pistol from his cross draw holster and smashed it across Coy's face -- causing him to drop the weapon. As almost a continuation of the same move, Mace slammed the barrel down on Dutch's knife holding arm. The force of the blow drove the blade into the board floor -- point first.

"You broke my arm!" Dutch shouted.

"If I didn't, it wasn't for lack of tryin'."

The judge took note of Truax and his ability to handle this situation as the barkeep produced a double-barrel shotgun from under the bar.

Coy held his face, blood streaming through his fingers, and looked

CHAPTER SIX

for his pistol as Truax stepped over and snatched it off the floor. Claxton saw the shotgun and said, "I don't think we'll be needing that, Jules."

The bartender glanced from Coy to Dutch and then back before he nodded and lowered his weapon.

Coy turned to Mace.

"Hey, who the hell are you?"

"A friend."

"You ain't no friend of mine," Coy said on unsteady feet.

Mace motioned to the two combatants.

"How long have you two known each other?"

It was Dutch who spoke up. "We been ridin' t'gether fer twenty years."

"Closer t' twenty-five," Coy said.

Mace looked at Coy.

"Would you say *he's* a friend."

"Damn right!"

"Well, I just kept you from killing your friend."

Coy realized what Mace had just said and looked at the two weapons the tall man held in his hands.

"You boys come t' town t' get drunk -- and fight?

"Sure. What else?" Dutch said. "I wouldn't have cut him."

"And I weren't goin' t' kill Dutch. That ol' hogleg don't even work half th' time."

Mace Truax spun the chambers of the pistol, executed the road-agent's-spin, cocked it, and fired it into the floor.

Coy was shocked.

Mace pulled on the end of Dutch's hair and whacked off a piece with the razor-sharp knife blade. Then turning to the barkeep, Mace said, "Put these somewhere safe -- but don't give 'em back until these two are ready to leave town."

"Will do."

"Why don't you help your friend find a doctor?" Mace suggested.

Coy and Dutch nodded, and headed out the door, sheepishly.

"And you boys do th' rest of your drinkin' an' all your fightin' -- somewheres else," the bartender called after them.

CHAPTER SIX

Judge Parker stepped aside to let them exit. The judge nodded his head to Cross. The Judge indicated Truax.

"Mr. Cross, please find out who that man is. I would like to talk to him -- tomorrow."

Claxton patted Mace on the back. "Nice work there."

Truax shrugged it off.

"Half of the job of an officer in the Army was to keep the enlisted men from killing each other when they got bored."

The bartender sat two more beers on the bar.

"On th' house," he said. He offered his hand to Mace. "Call me, Jules."

"Thanks," Mace and Landers echoed each other.

Mace raised his glass to the bartender, "Jules. I'm Mace."

Presley Cross stepped up to the bar, saying, "Excuse me, sir."

Get your copy of My Gavel and the Gun here through AMAZON.

TWO FREE E-BOOKS

[Murder in Muleshoe]
If you were murdered would they try to find the killer or plan him a parade?

[Guns Along The Rio]
In 1858, two fresh-off-the-ranch 17-year-olds join the Texas Rangers. What could possibly go wrong?

GO TO: http://eepurl.com/dKEi_Y

ABOUT THE AUTHOR

Jack R. Stanley is a native Texan born two blocks inside Texas and raised six blocks inside Arkansas in Texarkana, Arkansas/Texas. He received his B.F.A. from Texas Christian University in Ft. Worth in Radio-TV-Film. As an officer in the U.S. Army serving in Vietnam as a TV-Film Director, he was awarded the Bronze Star. He says when you're in a firefight and you have a camera when everybody else on both side have guns, you get to change your pants a lot.

After his military service he earned both his M.A. and his Ph.D. at the University of Michigan in Ann Arbor in Radio-TV-Film. He also received two of Michigan's most prestigious creative writing awards, The Hopwood Award, one for a one-act play and the second for a novel. His novel, Campus Confidential is available to Amazon.com in paperback.

Stanley's first academic position was TV Area Head at The University of Texas at Austin's Department of Radio-TV-Film. He later moved to deep south Texas and the Lower Rio Grande Valley for a challenging position with The University of Texas-Pan American. Here he taught Theatre-TV-Film for 30 years in the Department of Communication serving as Department Chair at U.T.P.A. for 11 years. He did take one year out to work for The University of Alaska Anchorage as a visiting professor. Back in Texas, Stanley directed for stage at The University Theatre, produced and directed fifteen student staffed, cast, and crewed feature films, writing most of the original screenplays. A very few of his credits are available on IMDB.com.

Stanley, more than 50 years happily married to his high school sweetheart, now lives in the Texas Panhandle where he writes his fiction and runs his blog, *www.TheFictionWritersNotebook.com*. His e-mail address is. Jacks@wrightbridgepress.com

ALSO BY THE AUTHOR
NOVELS

[Westerns]

Guns Along The Rio

West Of The Frio

A Hard Line Between The Rios

The Mormon Marshal

Along The Outlaw Trail

The Gavel and the Gun

13 Steps To Hell

Incident At Lajitats

Pancho's Pilot

Return to Redemption

Occurrence At Latigo

[Political Fiction]

The Reluctant President

The Reluctant Incumbent

The Reluctant Candidate

The Elected President

[Vietnam]

Through A Lens Darkly: Vietnam

[Mysteries]

Murder In Muleshoe

Corpse In Canyon

The Lovecraft Murders

Short Stories

TALES FROM THE ALASKAN GOLD RUSH

Klondike Justice

Dangerous Camp On The Kenai

The Winds of Skagway

Screenplays

6 and 10

The 7th Luger

Afternoon Delight

Angel's Revenge

Between Love And Murder

Blood Drive

Death Scene

The Defection of Grigori Dorsky

The Evil Eye

Fatty and Hearst

Gideon: The Horse That Saved Texas

Hell In Paradise

Hollowpoint

Holiday For An Assassin

Horse Thief Hollow

Incident A tLajitas

Love, Lust, & Life

Mom & Apple Pye

Pancho's Pilot

The Prometheus Peril

The Rape of Sarah Quinn

Reservations

River of Tears

Seven Reasons Why

The Thing About Love

The Texas Rattlesnake Murders

Too Good To Be True

The Vampire Rose

A Violent End

The Virgin Casanova

Plays

Antigone In Texas

Cyrano

The Last Virgin From Las Vegas

The Seven Keys

The Unwed Widow

Made in the USA
Monee, IL
24 September 2020